AMY'S CHOICE

MARCIA STRYKOWSKI

LUMINIS BOOKS

LUMINIS BOOKS
Published by Luminis Books
1950 East Greyhound Pass, #18, PMB 280
Carmel, Indiana, 46033, U.S.A.
Copyright © Marcia Strykowski, 2014

Cover art and design by Rachel A Marks.

Hardcover ISBN: 978-1-935462-08-8
Paperback ISBN: 978-1-935462-13-2

Printed in the United States of America

10 9 8 7 6 5 4 3 2 1

LUMINIS BOOKS

Meaningful Books That Entertain

For Bob, a good choice.

Praise for *Call Me Amy,* selected for Best Children's Books of the Year by Bankstreet College of Education:

"A wounded seal pup propels 13-year-old Amy Henderson into an unlikely alliance with an unusual older woman and a mysterious boy in a small Maine fishing village. Readers will cheer for Amy as she protects Pup, gains confidence, faces challenges, and comes up with an idea that could change not only the future of her village, but also her own life. With a skillful hand, Strykowski introduces us to a small town with memorable characters and the girl who could bring them all together."

—Anne Broyles, award-winning author of *Priscilla and the Hollyhocks*

"In a small town in Maine in the 1970's, Amy is standing on the brink of becoming a teenager. The events that will force her to discover who she is, what she is made of and how she wants others to perceive her are sweetly told through awkward teenage moments, the triumphs and sadnesses of that age and, ultimately, Amy's discovery of her own beliefs, strength and courage."

—Kathleen Benner Duble, acclaimed author of *The Sacrifice*

"Well-drawn, sympathetic characters and the developing spark between Amy and Craig combine to create a pleasant, satisfying read."

—*Kirkus Reviews*

"Strykowski ably depicts Amy's insecurity and self-doubt, Craig's bravura and pain, and Miss Cogshell's wisdom with a deft, convincing touch. In essence, Amy comes of age as she fights to find her voice in the outside world and shed some of her debilitating insecurity. Readers will cheer her on, and her splendid team too."

—*Booklist*

"*Call Me Amy* is a powerful read that should prove very hard to put down—highly recommended."

—*Midwest Book Review*

"Strykowski lovingly captures seaside Maine and the travails of adolescence in her quiet, sweet-natured debut novel."

—*Publishers Weekly*

"This character-driven novel is told from Amy's point of view. The protagonist grows throughout the story, from a shy loner to having two friends and speaking her mind in front of her adversaries at school as well as to the whole town. . . Amy is a reliable narrator and easily relatable."

—*School Library Journal*

"Having all the ingredients of first love, faith, loss and strength makes *Call Me Amy* unforgettable."

—*Feathered Quill Book Reviews*

Advance Praise for *Amy's Choice:*

"I enjoyed *Amy's Choice* just as much, if not more, than *Call Me Amy*. Although Strykowski's second book has the same timeless, wholesome feel as the first, Amy has evolved as she struggles with more mature situations. The setting of the small Maine coastal town is idyllic, and the reader is quickly and completely immersed in this community."

"The 1970s pop-culture references are fun... young readers will readily associate with Amy's struggles and triumphs in her relationships with family and friends, while mature readers will be gently nudged back to this period in their lives. These universal qualities make *Call Me Amy* and *Amy's Choice* a perfect choice for many types of readers."

"As a Youth Services Librarian, I enthusiastically recommend the *Amy* books to our young patrons as well as to a more adult audience. Because they can be enjoyed on so many levels, these novels are an ideal source of discussion for adult/child book groups."

—Patty Falconer, Hampstead Public Library

"Strykowski lets you see Amy's development, through the first person narrative and her interaction with other people. Like *Call Me Amy,* this novel does a great job of evoking the early '70s, so the reader can see what that time was like. The conflicts and learning experiences... are fairly timeless for kids working their way through the teen years and figuring out who they are as individuals. As an adult, I enjoyed reminiscing about those times and that era... ultimately, the novel is a great read for young teens."

—Kate Thomas, Librarian

Acknowledgments

Many thanks to Anne Broyles, Kathleen Benner Duble, Tracy Richardson, Derek Strykowski, and Marla Strykowski for helping me choose the right words. Also, thank you to everyone at Luminis Books. And as always, thank you to my family and friends for your love and support.

1

"HI, I'M AMY," I told the new girl, and from that moment on, our friendship blossomed. Those three little words turned the tide on my dreaded return to school. No longer was I scared right out of my lime-green sneakers to start alone, up at the huge, jam-packed high school.

That split second of bravery was how I met my new best friend: Caterina Elizabeth Fantino—a sturdy girl with long dark hair always in a braid and sparkly blue eyes behind round granny glasses. She was half Italian and half Irish and insisted that I call her Cat.

"It suits me, don't you think?" she'd said, when we first met in the library three weeks before school started.

I'd spent that whole summer of 1973 helping to get Port Wells' first library established. During the early weeks, while I unpacked books, filed cards, and organized shelves, Cat would come in and head for the big chair in the back reading room. She always smiled at me, and I'd smile back, of course, but that was all. Then, when Craig, the coolest guy in the world, told me he was leaving for Boston, I knew loneliness would be just around the corner. I decided to do something about it before it could strike me speechless. That's why I introduced myself to Cat on that same hot summer day.

Cat was a talker, and after about ten minutes, I felt like we'd known each other for years. "I love to read mysteries, play Clue, bake, and jump into the ocean for 30 seconds in the dead of winter," she said, quickly adding, "in that order." And then after a pause to catch her breath, she asked, "What do you like to do?"

For someone who'd always been shy, I felt surprisingly comfortable with Cat and soon told her all my interests as well, emphasizing mystery books and board games. I neglected to mention that most of my baking attempts were disasters and that the last place you'd find me in the dead of winter, or at any other time, was up to my neck in waves.

"We are two of a kind," she decided.

"And, you're not summer people, right? You're planning to stay?" I peeked up at my new friend and crossed my fingers behind my back. It wouldn't be the first time over the years that I'd met a kindred spirit, only to have them head for the city a month or so later.

"Definitely. Dad left his office job and bought himself a lobster boat. We're staying."

Yet even then, despite having finally made the perfect friend, I still missed Craig each and every minute. He was supposed to be gone only a short time, while his mom got treatment for her drinking problem. When he left, I think we both assumed he'd be back before school started.

AND NOW IT was September and our first day of school. Three weeks had passed since the day I'd met Cat and said goodbye to Craig. After breakfast, I found myself cheerfully grabbing my school supplies and actually looking forward to what the day might bring.

I practically hopped to the bus stop in my excitement to get there. But, of course, high school girls don't jump around like goobers, so I stuck to a slight bounce.

When I reached the bottom of our hill, I sprinted past the field and could soon make out Cat's familiar shape standing at the corner. So far, we'd mostly met up at the library, although I knew she lived in the white house with green shutters, a few doors up the road from the post office. With all the nice weather we'd been having, it was too nice to be indoors. We usually hung around the pier or took walks in our free time, when we weren't working in the library. We both volunteered there now—Cat on Saturdays and random weekdays, and me almost every day, except Sunday, when we were closed.

Unexpectedly, there seemed to be two people at the bus stop.

"Amy! Hi!" she shouted.

I waved back. The cute boy standing beside her was about the same height as Cat. He had dark wavy hair.

"This is Ricky," said Cat.

I looked from her to him, then back to her again.

"Remember, I told you I had brothers?" she added.

I gave him a hesitant smile and then turned my attention back to my friend. "I thought your brother was in college."

"That's my *older* brother. Joey went back to Colby last week. Ricky here," she gave her brother a playful punch in the elbow. "He's been in science camp the past three weeks." She rolled her eyes. "A tenth grader. Only ten months and six days older than me." Cat laughed and straightened to her full height. "We're having a race to see who ends up taller."

Ricky turned a little red, and I realized he hadn't yet uttered a word.

Pulling forth my new plan to be more sociable, I said, "How do you like Port Wells, so far?"

"It's pretty cool," he said. "I miss Portland, but the scenery's good here." He had a nice voice that made him even cuter than he already was, if that was possible. He adjusted his wire-rim glasses and looked out towards the road. I realized how nervous he, and maybe even Cat, must be. They'd never been in our school system, whereas I'd been with this bunch of kids forever.

Cat had mentioned how her mom had brought her into Portland to get new school clothes. Her jumper was plaid with princess seams and looked great on her. "I like your new outfit," I said.

"Thanks, your denim skirt's really cute."

I laughed and did a jumping jack, so she could see the split in my 'skirt'. "It's culottes!" Then I realized Ricky had turned back around and, feeling foolish, I immediately adopted a more mature pose.

Cat shifted her weight and peered in both directions. "Are we the only ones at this bus stop?"

"Yep, and it used to be only me."

"What about your sister? What grade is she in?"

"Nancy's in eleventh and refuses to ride the bus. She and her gang pack as many kids as they can into one of her friend's old station wagons."

"And that blond kid?" Cat asked. "The one you were with after your 4th of July speech?"

My mind went back to the day I first saw Cat, when I was up on stage at the picnic announcing my idea to turn my friend's house into a library. After spending a lot of time in Miss Cogshell's home before she died, I'd have done anything to save it from ruin. Cat had cheered and waved a small American flag in support of my idea. She and I hadn't actually talked, though, until several weeks after the picnic—and that day was a gold-star day for me. First, I had hugged Craig (yes, me, recently known as the nerd called Shrimp, had actually hugged a boy). And then I'd introduced myself to Cat that same day.

I realized she was still waiting for my answer.

"That was Craig." Now it was my turn to blush. "He's in Boston for a while." I was actually surprised she remembered seeing Craig. She must have watched me go straight from the stage to join him at the back of the crowd. Then again, he was kind of hard to miss, or forget, for that matter. He was really tall with hair the color of ripe corn and eyes that matched the ocean. I hadn't seen him since our goodbye, yet I still thought about him round the clock. There had been times I almost mentioned him to Cat, but I still found it painful to talk about the wonderful spring I'd had with him and Miss Cogshell. The three of us had taken care of an abandoned seal pup. And then, it was like all three of them just disappeared—poof! First, we released Pup back to the ocean, then Miss Cogshell died, and then Craig left, too. I guess I figured talking about him might jinx his return.

The smelly old bus pulled up, and on we got. With a friend to sit with, the ride to school didn't seem as long and boring. Ricky sat across from us.

"Enjoy your first day," I said when he left for the third floor and Cat and I headed for Room 202.

I stared after him. "Wow, I didn't realize your brother would be like that."

"Like what?" Cat turned to look at him. "You mean goofy?"

I decided to keep my mouth shut on that one. All I needed was for her to tell him I thought he was cute. "Isn't it great that we'll be in the same homeroom *and* English class?" I said to change the subject.

Some of the kids had really shot up over the summer. A few could easily have been mistaken for adults. Good ol' Pamela and Claire, the two girls who made my life miserable, were in several of my classes again. No matter. It would be easier to ignore them this year. I was busy with my own friend now.

EVERY DAY AFTER school, before my library shift, I swung by the post office. Kind of like the saying "watched pots never boil," I knew watched mail slots never produced letters, but still I checked, in hopes of a note from Craig. He was my best friend all last spring and summer and when he left for Boston three weeks, three days, and three hours earlier, he said he'd write, or at least try.

And then, after my unrewarding post office visit, I always went to the far end of the pier.

Cat didn't miss much. "What are you looking for out there all the time?" she said one day.

"Huh?"

"You're constantly watching the water."

"Oh, that. I'm looking for an old friend. Last spring…" I proceeded to tell her all about Pup, the little harbor seal Craig and I had nursed back to health.

"It was so sad when we said goodbye and let him return to the sea a couple of months ago." Then I brightened. "I've seen him. Twice now. And better still, he has a friend." I smiled at Cat. "Pup and I both found new friends."

"That is way cool," said Cat. "Maybe I can get to know Pup, too."

I glanced back out to sea. "Let's hope so." It would be great if Cat could meet Pup *and* Craig. But would Craig ever return to Port Wells?

2

"YA KNOW, RICKY has a crush on you," said Cat the following Saturday morning as we were shelving books at the library.

I glanced over my shoulder to make sure Mrs. Baldwin, our head librarian, was busy elsewhere. "Right," I said, kind of flattered, but disbelieving.

Cat tossed her thick braid back over her shoulder and spun around to stare at me. "He does. He won't admit it, of course, but he's constantly asking me questions about you—What's her favorite color? What's her favorite book? What kind of candy does she like? I finally screamed at him—ask her yourself! Gosh, ever since that first day he saw you at the bus stop, it's like he can't think of anything else." Cat shrugged. "He was never much of a talker before, so I guess it's a good thing."

I was stunned. That explained Thursday. It had taken Ricky a half hour to ask me which I liked better—

baseball or basketball. When I told him they were equal, he seemed relieved, like I had passed some big test. I almost considered telling Cat that my heart belonged to Craig, but no matter how I figured out the words in my head, they sounded way too corny.

LATER THAT AFTERNOON, Cat said, "It looks like rain. Why don't we hang out at my house for a while?"

"Sure." I was eager to see the inside of the white house with green shutters. Old Man Turner had lived there for years, but he never opened up for company. Then, after he died, the house stood empty for another couple of years while his heirs argued about what to do with it. Lucky for me, they finally sold it to the Fantinos and I got a best friend out of the deal.

The library closed at two o'clock on Saturdays and by then the waves were choppier than ever. The sky was gray as a gull's wings and filled with the scent of wet kelp. We crunched along the gravel drive leading to Cat's house. Mr. Fantino's shiny red pick-up truck was parked to one side beside a stack of lobster traps. I took in the shape of the house as we moved closer.

"I love that neat pointed section in the middle," I said, looking at the roof.

"That's the boys' loft up there," said Cat matter-of-factly.

A tarnished ship bell hung by the door. Cat gave the cord a few swings, and it rang loudly. "Wanna try it? Nobody's home."

I glanced at her dad's truck and then remembered her mom had a car, too.

"My parents went into Rockland today for an exhibit," explained Cat.

I closed my eyes and took a big breath of salty air. Then I knocked the pendulum back and forth, each time impressively louder.

"Okay, enough!" Cat covered her ears, and we both laughed.

The first thing I saw when we entered the living room was a big, shiny black piano. "Oh, cool! Who plays this?"

"I do." Cat sighed. "I didn't mention it in my list of favorite things because I hate to practice." She patted the piano fondly. "It's growing on me."

A mason jar filled with broken sea glass was displayed on top of the piano, along with family photos. Music books were spread out on the bench and colorful, striped afghans swallowed up the sofa. Everything looked comfortable and lived-in, like the Fantinos had always been there.

After climbing a ship-style ladder in the front foyer, we peeked into Ricky's room.

"The empty part is Joey's," said Cat. "Most of his stuff is with him at college."

On Ricky's side, there were science posters on the wall and a large half-built model ship. Empty chip bags littered the carpet. A pile of dirty clothes was partially stuffed under the bed. It felt weird to be in a boy's room. My mother would have a field day cleaning this house. I looked around in curious amazement.

"Yep, he's a slob." Cat laughed. "And he'll kill me if he finds out I let you see his mess."

The stack of books I checked out to him two days before was on the floor. Kurt Vonnegut's recent bestseller, *Breakfast of Champions,* teetered on top. "When does he get a chance to read all these?" I asked.

"Hah. He doesn't read most of them. He just likes to visit you."

My face got warm as I considered this possibility.

We climbed back down from the loft and moved on to Cat's room, which was—except for a scraggly troll collection—all pink and perfect.

"Whoa, pretty!" I said.

"Don't make fun. As soon as I'm allowed to cover this paint, I'm going for something wild and dramatic, like avocado or burnt orange."

"That makes more sense," I said with a grin.

12

Cat rummaged through a pile of stuff on her bureau. "Look at this," she said, slipping a green and orange plastic ring onto her finger.

"Cool! I have a Rat Fink ring, too. Mine is a yellow rat on a blue ring. Hmm, I wonder where it is." A few years back, the rings had been a real fad in Port Wells. You could buy them at Al's for a dime. All the kids had them. We'd wear them to school, and if the teacher wasn't looking, we'd pull the chubby rats off their ring holders and play with them under our desk lids.

Cat picked up one of her long-haired trolls. "I've got a few of these from when I was little, too."

I laughed. "Me, too. My favorite troll has orange hair and is dressed like a wizard."

We hung around Cat's room for a while longer, until we got hungry.

We were in the kitchen finishing up ice cream sundaes, when Ricky arrived home from his newspaper route.

"Is it raining yet?" said Cat.

"Nope, still holding . . ." Ricky did a double-take in my direction. "Oh, hi, Amy."

"Hi," I ducked my head quickly, surprised to feel my face get hot.

I stood up and brought my dish to the sink, preparing to leave. Cat stood in my path.

"Ricky, Amy wants to know about science camp," she said with a mischievous grin. "How about you fill her in while I start my homework? Is that okay, Amy?"

"Sure. I've got to go soon, anyway." I sat back down and felt my face redden again. Why did he have to be so cute?

Ricky got himself some ice cream and plunked it down across the table from me. "What would you like to know?"

"Well, like, what did you do there? I'm figuring you didn't swim and boat and do the usual camp stuff."

"Right. Some of that, but lots of classes in science, too. We'd fire off rockets and shoot potatoes out of homemade cannons." Ricky became animated, conducting with his ice cream spoon, as he described several hazardous situations.

"Wow, sounds dangerous."

Ricky laughed. "Yeah, I guess it does. There were some close calls, but it was a blast, and we were pretty careful."

"Yes, blowing things up must be a real blast. I'll keep my distance though, thanks."

After Ricky finished his ice cream, I decided it was time to go. Ricky got up, too. We went out the back door together and headed towards my house. I smiled at the thought of being escorted home. A wet drop landed on my nose. I could actually see a few sprinkles of rain bounce off the ground. Then I felt them, hard. Huh?

"Oh, cool," said Ricky. "Hail!"

I grinned. "I like hail, too. I haven't seen it in years." As I spoke, the mini clusters of ice enlarged until they were pelting us left and right. "Ouch!" We both couldn't stop laughing. I tried to duck between them while Ricky attempted to catch them in the palm of his hand. "We're surrounded!"

When my house was in view, I finally said between gasps, "You'd better go home."

With noticeable reluctance, Ricky agreed. He kept calling back, "Bye, Amy!" and I did the same. Well, except with his name in place of mine. We were both still laughing between shouts.

Alone, I hiked up the rest of the hill to our big, old Victorian house. On a gray, wet day like today, it could almost look haunted through the pines, but once inside it was cheery enough, and thanks to Mom, neat as a pin.

"Yippee!" I could hear Nancy's scream before I even opened the door to go inside. My sister came leaping down the stairs. "I made it! Yay me!"

I shook off the dampness and gave her a puzzled look. "Cheerleading?" Since trying out last week, Nancy hadn't shut up about how much she wanted to make the team.

"Yes! I am going to be *so* popular." She did a little twirl. "Everyone will want to be me!"

"I don't want to be you," I said.

She looked at me with a condescending smile. "Feel free to thank me, dear sister; *you* might even rise up a couple of levels, just by association."

I gave a snort. Luckily, she didn't act quite this stuck-up in public. I covered my ears as she broke into another cheer.

"Here we go, Whalers, here we go!" She clapped out the beat with her hands.

Well, one thing was true, she certainly was loud enough to be heard at both ends of the football field.

3

BY THE SECOND week of September, it was harder to picture my old friend, Craig. Sure, he had that thick blond hair, but were his eyes always blue, or were they sometimes flecked with green? Did I still come up to an inch below his shoulder? And exactly how did his voice sound? Was it deeper now?

Nancy teased me about my constant trips to the post office. "Anything from Cutie Pie yet?" she'd say.

Most of the time I could ignore her, although once I regrettably shrieked out, "Craig promised he'd write to me, and he will!" As soon as I said it, my eyes filled with tears.

"Sor-*ry!*" Nancy gave me a light punch in the arm.

On the other hand, Ricky's cheerful face was always easy to picture. His eyes were dark as charcoal and his hair matched. And he had a chipped tooth, the one to the right of his two front teeth.

EARLY SUNDAY MORNING, Cat and I dangled our bare feet over the end of the pier. Despite a chilly breeze, the dark sea was smoother than usual, interrupted only by swirling ripples. We watched a small schooner glide across to the island until it faded into mist.

"Ya know, Amy, I didn't think I wanted to come here. Both Ricky and I gave my parents kind of a hard time about moving to Port Wells." Cat rolled her eyes. "We thought we'd be lonely and, I don't know, maybe we were a little afraid, but now I'm wicked glad we did. Our whole family seems happier here—more relaxed."

I smiled at her. "I'm glad, too."

Beyond Cat, on distant rocks, a lone fisherman cast his line far out to sea. Lobster buoys bobbed here and there. Seagulls swooped in and out of the gentle waves, doing their own fishing.

"And the library," continued Cat. "Gosh, it's like I was born to work there. I used to envy the older girls who shelved books at the Portland Library. I never thought I'd soon be doing the same thing. It sounds stupid, but I love the smell of old books and to imagine all the kids who read them before me."

"That's not stupid at all," I said. "Did you see the copy of *Huckleberry Finn* on display? It's from 1885!"

"Yeah. I was thinking of setting up a few books to go with it. Classics that were popular a hundred years ago and still are today. Books like *Little Women* and *Alice in Wonderland*."

I got caught up in Cat's enthusiasm. "Oh, and how about *The Wizard of Oz*? That was from back around that time, too. Those authors would freak out to know their work is still so fashionable."

"They'd be shocked by the new stuff that's out now," said Cat.

"Yeah, what would they think of Ponyboy and the rest of the Greasers gang? Did you know that author was only 16 years old when she wrote *The Outsiders*?" I sighed. "Not much older than us."

"You're really good in English, Amy. Maybe someday your name will be among them."

"Ha," I said. "Fat chance." I thought about the kitten story I had written in fifth grade and how embarrassed I was when the teacher read it aloud to the whole class.

My hair was flying all over the place from the strong salty breezes. I grabbed a clump and stuffed it into the back of my collar and then peered out to sea.

From the direction of Wàwàckèchi Island, a strange contraption came into view. The small dingy chugged towards us, making its way slowly through the fog. *Was it a boat?* What else could it be? A triangle structure jutted up from the midsection—too misshapen and dark to be a sail. I nudged Cat, and together we watched it draw near.

"What in the world *is* that?" She leaped up for a better view.

I didn't budge; not sure of who or what was in that boat. There appeared to be a hunched figure sitting in front of the oddly shaped cargo.

With one last splat, the boat slid up onto our little beach. An old man unfolded himself, placed a rubber boot onto the sand, and then climbed the rest of the way over the edge of the craft. He gathered up all his strange goods—stuff wrapped in garbage bags—and headed for the pier.

Cat ran over to meet him. "Want some help?"

I thought he was going to ignore her, until he mumbled through his whiskers, "I'll manage." He cleared his throat—almost like he wasn't used to speaking out loud. Up close, he wasn't as elderly as he first appeared—weathered, yet quite nimble.

With a shrug of her shoulders, Cat came back to sit beside me. She sat at an angle in order to watch and report.

"What's he doing?" I whispered, not wanting us both to be gawking at him.

"It's an easel. He must be a painter."

Now I had to turn around, too—I loved to watch painters. And he certainly looked the part with his scruffy white beard. I stood up to see him better.

We kept inching closer to where he had his equipment spread out. Pretty hard to ignore us at that point, so eventually the old man sighed and turned his steady gaze on us.

"The name's Finn," he said. "Haven't been off the island in a while."

"How long have you lived there?" I asked.

"Oh, 'bout thirty years or so, I'd say. I grew up here, on the mainland, but Wàwàckèchi Island and its lighthouse kept calling me home."

Cat gave a puzzled expression. "The lighthouse called you?"

"Yep, a few decades back, there was a small ad posted for a lighthouse keeper. Being a deserted kind of island, what with only a handful of houses and all, not too many people relished the idea of taking up the position."

Cat and I looked at each other, and then I said, "I'd think a lot of people would love that job. Watching the storms come in and getting to flash the light and blow the horn."

Finn chuckled. "Oh, yeah, it's all romanticized nowadays. But what about all the other empty hours? It's not for everyone. Most lighthouses have switched to motorized methods. Even Wàwàckèchi went auto last year. That's why I get to spend time away now."

A thought occurred to me. "Did you know Miss Cogshell? Before you moved to the island?"

"Cogshell." He stroked his whiskers a minute and then grinned. "You must mean Sylvie."

"Yes! Sylvia Cogshell." There was nothing better than to discover yet another person who remembered my beloved mentor with fondness.

"She and my eldest sister used to chum around back in the day. And believe you me, she was a character even then." He turned to take a long look at Miss Cogshell's small weathered home, from the widow's walk on top, down to the little sign in the window that read Port Wells Public Library. His face took on a sad appearance. "Both gone now. But, yep, she was a sharp one."

"Her house is our new library," I said, stating the obvious.

Finn continued to organize his paints and then he squeezed a few dollops onto his palette. He unfolded a small metal stool and positioned himself on it in front of the easel. His dark eyes gazed out from leathery skin as though seeing the island in the distance for the first time. I looked too, and saw the early morning fog had melted away like magic. Finn dashed a few light lines of charcoal onto a fresh white canvas.

"Are you going to paint Wàwàckèchi?" asked Cat.

"Yep. And if you two stop jabbering, I just might get started before nightfall."

4

ALMOST DAILY, EACH time I returned to the pier, Finn was there, too. "Already painted up about all that's on the island. Might's well make use of the view from over here for a while."

I checked his progress and praised his beautiful work. The way he caught the light almost brought tears to my eyes.

One blustery day, after Cat showed up at the pier, the two of us left Finn to his work and wandered over to the library. It was almost time to open anyway. Since the town could only afford to pay Mrs. Baldwin for part-time hours, we didn't open on Mondays, Wednesdays, and sometimes Fridays, until after school got out.

"Uh, oh," I said, just before we reached the path. Cat stopped and turned to look up the road in the direction I was staring. Pamela and Claire were headed our way, and already I could hear them discussing us.

"Here come the bookworms," said Claire.

"How fitting," shrieked Pamela. "Shrimp has a worm for a friend." She doubled over with a fit of laughter.

Because I was short for my age, the nickname Shrimp had been with me for more years than I wanted to count. I thought I'd got rid of it when I stood up to these snots in front of Craig at the end of the school year. Although I guess now that Craig wasn't around, the name had returned.

Pamela could barely get her next words out, she was laughing so hard. "Fat worms are called slugs!"

"Shrimp and Slug!" echoed Claire.

I clenched my fists. I was so mad I couldn't breathe.

Pamela peered at Cat. "What *is* your name anyway?"

"My name is Cat," Cat said in a clear, confident voice.

Claire burst out in new giggles. "Not a slug, a fat cat!"

Cat shrugged and moved towards the library, but I was cemented in place.

"Love your shoes," said Pamela to me. "I want to buy a pair like those." Both girls turned away amidst gales of laughter, while I tugged at my bell bottoms, hoping to cover up more of my worn-out lime-green sneakers.

"Just ignore them," said Cat, over her shoulder.

We turned in at the library while those two ducked into the post office.

My breath came in short bursts as I unclenched my fists. "I can't stand them."

"It's not worth the hassle," said Cat. "Who cares what they think?" I looked at Cat in amazement as she casually straightened a wooden buoy that hung by the library door. How could she let their cruel words slide off her so easily, like a lobster shedding last year's shell?

We waited on the back steps for Mrs. Baldwin to come and let us in. And, as usual, we waited and waited. I tried to copy Cat—tried to forget how mean Pamela and Claire had been.

"Ricky was asking about you again," said Cat with a bored sigh. She yanked out three long strands of crabgrass from under the lilac bush and proceeded to braid them together. "He wanted to know what time you get out of work."

I felt my face go warm. "What did you tell him?"

"That you get out about five-thirty." Cat spun around to look at me. "Why? Should I not have told him?"

"No, that's fine." I shrugged as though it was no big deal. "I hope you'll get to meet Craig. He's a cool kid."

Cat slammed her palm against her forehead. "Now I get it. You're stuck on Craig," she said. "Duh, I guess I am a slug—kind of slow." She laughed.

How could Cat kid about the rotten thing Pamela had said? Cat wasn't a slug. I started to deny her comment about Craig, but I knew it was too late. "Yeah, we were pretty close. Don't tell anyone."

"Yeah, I won't tell Ricky either. Because, ya know, he's cool, too. And well, in case. . .."

I knew she meant in case Craig didn't come back. I got up from the steps and moved away from Cat, glanced towards the ocean. "He'll be back," I said.

FINALLY MRS. BALDWIN arrived, breathless.

"Had some errands to do in Thomaston," she shouted as she strode up the path. She slipped her key into the lock, and we all went in and opened windows—our routine to get out the musty smells.

"I've decided," said Mrs. Baldwin, "that you girls are dependable enough to carry a key, as well. That way you won't have to wait outside in the cold, if per chance I am delayed." She pursed her lips. "Although of course I am never one to be tardy."

I gave a little grin, not sure if the staid Mrs. Baldwin had attempted a joke at her own expense. She was late every other day.

"I've made you a copy." She pulled the key out of her purse with great flair and handed it to me. "I've put it on a string. Now don't lose it."

I looked at Cat. "We can share it."

Cat threw her arms up and put her hands into a stop position. "No way. Everybody, including apparently Mrs. Baldwin, knows I'd lose my own head if it wasn't attached."

I shrugged. "Okay, then." I pulled the string over my head and felt a heightened sense of responsibility.

I LEFT THE library that day at five thirty-five and looked in both directions. No Ricky in sight. Mrs. Baldwin and Cat had already gone home. A strong wind got hold of the door and swung it wide. I pulled it back and locked the door securely; then, after pulling the string over my head again, I stuffed my new key inside my sweatshirt. Dark storm clouds rolled in, and the air smelled extra fishy. The once sunny day suddenly looked to be hours later than it was. Last time I remembered seeing the sky change that quickly, we'd been in for quite the thunder storm. The sound of surf and rattle of stones in the undertow filled the damp salt air. I could see Finn loading his equipment into the boat.

"Wait!" I broke into a run. "You can't get to the island in this weather."

"Yep, rain coming," was all he said when I reached the pier.

The wind whipped up and knocked over Finn's easel. Luckily his canvas was already packed. I watched him grab up the stand, fold it flat and then step into his boat.

"Stay over!" What was I saying? Would Mom and Dad even want this unkempt stranger to sleep in our house? They *did* like helping people out.

I was surprised Finn hadn't known a storm was coming with all his weather monitoring as a lighthouse keeper. He usually kept to the island on those days. "Do you have to be at the lighthouse?"

"Nope. The lighthouse is secure. A young Coast Guard chap has been staying there, keeping an eye on things. Only temporarily, to make sure all the automatic equipment is working shipshape."

"Great. Then you can stay?"

He shook his head. "That wouldn't work for me." And I realized he was too shy to impose. "I'm used to roughing it," he added.

"Maybe in the library?" The shiny new key, cold as an ice cube, pressed against my skin.

"Then I'd be your responsibility. If I hadn't got so caught up trying to get the angle of this boat right, I would've watched the weather better. No, I'll mosey along." We both glanced up at the storm clouds and then towards the island. Trouble was, there was no island. The fog had completely swallowed it up.

Finn climbed back out of the boat. "Whoo-ee, that fog set in quick. Might's well try out that old woodshed in back of the library."

We dragged the boat further up to the edge of the sand. Finn used some sort of fisherman's knot to secure the unattached end of his boat line to a stump. Then he gathered up his trash-bag-covered canvases and easel. I carried the paint box.

"There might be spiders," I said.

He chuckled. "Used to that, I am."

An open padlock was looped through to keep the door of the woodshed closed. Rust made it difficult to pry apart. After we got the old lock unstuck and used the last of the light to clear a sleeping area, I dashed home for supplies.

Within minutes, I had collected an air mattress, old bike pump, flashlight, large can of pork and beans, two packages of my favorite Twinkies, and an apple.

"What in heaven's name are you doing?" said Nancy. She strolled through the kitchen, filing her nails, still wearing her red cheerleading outfit. I wouldn't be surprised if she slept in that thing.

"I'm just really hungry," I answered, holding back a grin.

5

IT WORKED OUT well enough. In fact I'd say Finn actually got attached to the old woodshed. Two days later, he made a trip to the island for extra provisions in order for him to stay over more often, even in good weather.

"Might's well take advantage of that Coast Guard fellow while he's here," Finn said. "I'd like to get a couple more canvases filled before my fingers are too raw to hold a paintbrush." He had finished the first painting of the island, along with another one of the mainland. Now, on early mornings, he turned his easel around again, back towards the island to capture the sunrise.

After school, I always checked Finn's progress before taking my two-hour shift at the library.

"I'm getting a lot more done by not commuting," he said with a laugh. "And I sure do appreciate those canned goods that keep appearing on the step." Finn nodded, and I could see his wheels turning. "How about you and your pal come over to the island for a clambake? Should be just enough room in my little boat."

"Will we get to tour the lighthouse?"

"Yep."

"That sounds great!" I'd always wanted to know what the towering lighthouse was like on the inside. "Cat should be able to go on a Sunday morning. Her family usually goes to Saturday night mass instead," I said.

Realizing it was time for my work shift, I sprinted back to the library while trying to figure out how I would get permission for such an adventure. My mother didn't always like boats. Or strangers.

AS I STRAIGHTENED out the picture book area, Mrs. Baldwin paused by my side. I propped up a well-loved copy of *Blueberries for Sal* to display on the top shelf.

"Oh, this reminds me," she said. "I thought we should start a new program. A story time for all the youngsters who come in on Saturday mornings. Would you be able to be in charge of that, Amy?"

Other than a few quick book checkouts, I hadn't really been around little kids since I was one myself. Kids were always so bouncy, and worst of all, way too honest. In fact, the last time I checked out a book for a husky second grader, I had given him my usual line about how he needed to have it back in two weeks. What did he do in response? He stuck his tongue out at me!

I swallowed and then answered Mrs. Baldwin. "Sure." I was already petrified.

Then I thought of a better solution. "I think Cat's been looking for a new project. She said she'd like to contribute something more stimulating than shelving books. And she *loves* kids." I babbled nonstop. "Cat said she's always the ring leader of her little cousins. She—"

"All right, all right, I believe you," said Mrs. Baldwin. "We'll give it a try."

And so it was decided. With her agreement, Cat would be the new storyteller on Saturday mornings. Whew, that was close.

Working at the library was cool because I got to do most of my homework while I waited between patrons. And then my nights were free.

Ricky had made a habit of coming around after his paper route, shortly before I left.

"If you got here earlier, I wouldn't have to kick you out each day at closing," I said with a laugh when he came in on Wednesday. He never even looked at the books. Did he really stop by only to see me?

Ricky flushed red.

I felt my own face get hot as I realized I'd embarrassed him. "Sorry, I didn't mean to criticize."

"No, you didn't," he said. "I mean. . ." He fidgeted with his glasses. "Can I walk you home?" he blurted.

"Oh. Ah, sure. I guess so. . ." I grabbed my books and sweater and locked up quickly.

A few steps past the door, Ricky stopped and looked back. "Ya know, you really could use a sign."

I peered at my library sign, stuck to the inside of the window. It had taken me forever. Each letter was a different bright rainbow color—nice and neat. "What's wrong with my sign?"

"Oh." Ricky flushed again. "Did you make that? It's er, nice." Ricky pushed his glasses up and considered the sign again. "I was thinking of a real, I mean, ya know, a *real* sign."

I made a face at my sign and studied it a minute. "Yep, you're right. Crayons on paper doesn't quite cut it. Except there's not much money in the library budget, like none at all. Lucky for us, people keep dropping off more book donations."

"I'm pretty good with my hands, with making stuff out of wood." Ricky's eyes lit up as he arched his arms high above his head. "A nice pine sign, or maybe oak, over the front door—with Port Wells Public Library all carved into it." He paused. "Or we could use stencils. You could help with that part, if you want. First, I'll sand it and put a base coat on. After it's done I'll weatherproof it with sealer."

"Sounds nice, but the library can't pay for it."

"No problem. I'll do it for free."

I grinned at Ricky. "Looks like Port Wells will be getting a new library sign."

Back on our way again, we hiked through the long grasses of the field that stretched out beyond the pier. Unlike for the 4th of July picnic, nobody kept the area mowed during the colder months. The pungent odor of marshy mud, washed by the tides, hung heavy in the air.

"Here, let me carry those," Ricky said abruptly. He took my books. I was too surprised to protest and instead attempted small talk. Trouble is I couldn't think of a single thing to say.

Then Ricky said, "Cat's super excited about running the Saturday story times."

"Yeah, that sure worked out great." I laughed. "Right up her alley!"

"She wants to be a teacher, you know."

I nodded.

Ricky looked thoughtful. "I'm not sure what I want to be—maybe a doctor or some kind of scientist."

"You'd be good at either of those," I said.

"It would be great to help people," Ricky continued. "Maybe cure a disease or something. How about you? What do you want to be?"

For years I'd been telling people I didn't know the answer to that question. When I was little, I used to make lists of possible professions with pluses and minuses beside them. Such as singer—love music, can't carry a tune. Dancer—fun, probably too clumsy. And then over the last few months, I figured I might be a librarian. Therefore, it surprised me when I suddenly announced, "I'm going to be a writer."

"Oh, cool," said Ricky. "What will you write?"

Still shocked by my career choice, I felt my face get warm. I mean hadn't I practically denied any interest in writing, to Cat, just the other day? "I'm not sure yet. It's kind of a new idea."

We fell into a comfortable silence.

Suddenly, a great blue heron, startled, flapped its way out of the marsh area beyond the field. We watched its long-beaked silhouette soar out to sea. Skinny twig legs stretched behind as the bird faded into the distance. Ricky and I exchanged happy smiles for the unspoken privilege of witnessing nature at its best.

Unlike when I used to walk with Craig, Ricky and I had a similar pace and stride. I didn't always have to run a few steps to catch up with him.

We didn't say much else on the way home. I was too concerned that Nancy might be peering out at us from her bedroom window as we trudged up the hill. If she asked about Ricky, the way she used to ask about Craig, I'm not sure what I would say. It was slowly dawning on me that he might want to be my boyfriend or something, and I wasn't sure I was ready for all that romantic stuff yet. And if I *was* ready, shouldn't I be with Craig? I grabbed my books back, said thanks, and dashed inside. From the safety behind the drape of the living room window, I watched Ricky make his way back down through the woods to the road.

6

I COULD BARELY sleep the night before our excursion to Wàwàckèchi Island. As it turned out, Mom and Dad had known Finn for ages as the 'lighthouse keeper on the island.' They'd even heard of mysterious good deeds he'd done over the years. Mom had talked to Cat's mother, and they both agreed it would be okay for the two of us to go with him, as long as we stuck together and got home before dark.

Good thing I got up early, because as it was, I had to wait forever for Nancy to get out of the bathroom. I put my ear up against the keyhole. Absolute silence.

"Are you in there staring at yourself in the mirror again?" I said.

"No, I am not." Another two minutes went by.

"Well, what *are* you doing?"

"Right now I'm applying lipstick, which is very difficult to do if I have to keep answering you."

"Think maybe you could do that in your room? Ya know, in front of your vanity mirror?"

I heard a big sigh through the keyhole. Suddenly, the door sprung open and I almost fell into the bathroom. Instead, I bumped into Nancy. She had an armful of make-up equipment that landed all over the floor.

"Ahh!" she shrieked.

I started to grab a jar of Noxzema Skin Cream.

"Don't touch! I'll pick everything up myself."

I crept into the bathroom and locked the door behind me. It took her a while to collect all her stuff. I waited until I heard her door close before I dared come back out.

I RACED THROUGH breakfast and then met Cat at the library. The sky was a vivid blue with puffy white clouds. Fragrant sea breezes carried the soft aroma of pines.

"Perfect day for a boat ride!" she said in greeting. We both had on sweatshirts and jeans.

"You got eight?" I asked. We checked our watches. Mine was one of those with changeable plastic straps where there was a snap on each side of the watch face and you could swap colors depending on your mood that day. I'd had it for a couple of years, so the lime-green and yellow bands were starting to wear out.

"Yep, it's eight," agreed Cat, looking at her sturdy brown-strapped watch.

We crossed the yard to pause at the woodshed. I put my ear to the dusty window. "Maybe he's still asleep."

"A date's a date," said Cat. She rapped at the door. No answer.

Before long, Finn's whiskered face came out of the outhouse across from the woodshed, on the other side of the yard. "All set," he said.

"We thought you were still catnapping."

"No, no, no. I've been down scrubbing up the boat. No more seaweed and guck in it. Even the seats are wiped down clean for you ladies." Finn chuckled. "Come on down to my yacht."

The three of us strolled to the pier. The raucous screams of gulls hunting for their breakfast interrupted the otherwise silent morning.

We climbed into Finn's tidy boat, barely fitting.

"Since you're just a bit of a thing, Amy, you sit at the tip."

Cat gave a snort. "I'll weigh down the middle."

Finn shook his head and grinned. "You, young lady, will be the rose between the oarlocks." Cat and I settled onto our seats while the boat rocked.

"I'll take up the rear to steer this here motor," said Finn. "You've each got a life cushion under your seat. Grab hold of it if a tidal wave hits."

"Or maybe we'll hit a whale." Cat said, laughing.

I faced backward and could see them both sitting forward, looking towards me. As we perched there, ready for take-off, wobbling in the water, my stomach felt funny, like it always did with motion. I reached down to check where my flotation cushion was located.

Finn yanked the motor's cord into life and shouted, "Yee ha, off we go!" His face was flushed with happiness. I was glad he felt comfortable enough to show us his 'hut' as he called his residence. The engine roared. Refreshing sprays of water surrounded us as we darted in and out between colorful buoys, across to the island.

We pulled up onto a little beach, trooped through some pine groves, and eventually came out on the other side of the island. At one edge, the huge lighthouse climbed high into the clouds. I felt smaller than ever as I gazed up to its top.

Lighthouses had always fascinated me. The foghorn whistle wasn't so different from a train whistle. Both had low melancholy cries that sounded haunted in the night. They let those of us at rest know that others were out there traveling by sea or rail. I could imagine the excitement on board a big ship during a storm. Waves crashing on wind-tossed seas and then—land ho—the flashing beams of the big light saying: rocks ahead! Come no closer! Or, if help was needed, the ship's captain might send a small boat out towards the welcoming glow.

"Here we are. Home sweet home," said Finn.

"Where do you stay?" said Cat. We both looked in every direction.

Finn motioned for us to follow him behind a thick clump of trees. An old shack blended right into the landscape. A rain barrel was tucked around one corner of it and a woodpile around the other.

"This here's the keeper's house." Finn laughed. "More run down than it used to be, but it will do. Rather than throw me out when they automated my job, they let me stay on with a free room." Finn scratched his whiskers. "Before we go inside, we'll get the blaze for our clambake going." He led us along a short path to another small beach.

"And then we'll visit the lighthouse, right?"

"Hold your horses, there, Amy. All in due time."

Finn deftly flicked a match into the fire pit. Smooth stones lined the bottom of the hole. He stirred the shrinking sparks with a stick. We watched the flames increase a moment, and then retraced our footsteps down the path until we reached Finn's home, entering through a rickety door.

The first room held a woodstove, straight-backed chair, rusty tray table, and a small refrigerator. Beyond the cozy kitchen was a bigger room. A tall easel and stacks of canvases filled one corner. Tubes of paint littered the floor. The smell of burnt wood mixed with turpentine filled the air. A saggy mattress covered with a worn brown comforter was stuffed against the other wall.

However, what really drew my eye was straight ahead—the whole wall was window glass with an uninterrupted view of the ocean beyond. I had never seen the Atlantic from quite this perspective. Blue and more blue as far as my eyes could see.

"This is so cool."

Finn left to tend the fire every once in a while. Cat and I couldn't stop watching the water view. Being further out from the mainland, we were hoping to see a huge tanker pass by.

"Woo, doggie. Yep, those stones are glowing." Finn was back from his last check. "Next we've got to collect a bunch of wet seaweed."

"And then the lighthouse?" I said.

Finn laughed as we followed him back outside to collect seaweed.

"Yuck," said Cat, taking careful steps when we neared water. "We're not going to eat algae, are we?"

"Nope, that's optional, you'll see." Now that the fire was almost out, Finn swept ashes from the hot stones and let them fill in the spaces between.

We each grabbed a bunch of soggy seaweed and placed our clumps over the stones. Finn brought out a big bowl of clams. He laid them between layers of moist brown seaweed, along with a few potatoes, carrots, and an onion. Then he went down to his little dock.

Finn tugged at a large piece of tarp that hung over the side of the wharf. It was drenched with sea water. He tossed it over the mound of food. "This will seal in the heat," he said.

"I don't really like seafood," I whispered to Cat. "I've got a package of Twinkies in my knapsack, just in case."

Cat rolled her eyes. "I love fish. I could eat it all day."

Our meal would take a few hours to cook. We went back inside. Cat continued to examine every inch of the two-room cabin. "Are these canvases all used?" she said. "Can we see them?"

Finn nodded, blushing. It always amazed me. Could an old guy like him really be so uncomfortable about his talents? Still? At his age? I'd always hoped I'd outgrow my insecurities by the time I was an adult.

Cat pulled out canvas after canvas. She held them by the edges and carefully displayed them against the walls and windows of the room.

I could only gape. I moved from one painting to the next, each one more breathtaking than the last. "You know," I said, at last. "You really should share these. People would love to see them."

Finn gave a slight grin, still surprisingly humble at the attention. "I was thinking of painting over most of them," he said. "A cheap way to get new canvas. A layer or two of white gesso, and they're good to go."

"No," shouted Cat. "You can't wreck these!"

"How about if you have an exhibit?" I suggested. "If you sell one painting, you can buy new supplies with the money you get."

"Nah. Nobody wants these. I'm no Wyeth. I tried to sell a few back in the day, but no takers. Course that was some time ago." Finn scratched his whiskered chin and shook his head. "I just like shoving a brush full of paint across where once there was nothing."

I looked at Finn until I got him to look me straight back in the eye. "They're beautiful," I said quietly. "I'd buy them all, right now, if I could."

Finn grinned and brushed me away like I was a pesky mayfly. "You keep it up, and my head will be too swollen to fit through this door." He pushed a pile of canvases back against the wall, their scenes out of view. Cat and I helped him stack the rest of the paintings.

"Can we go to the top of the lighthouse, now?" I couldn't wait much longer.

Finn chuckled. "Well, since it's at least the fourth time you've asked, I reason we'll have to."

7

UP CLOSE, THE light house tower appeared absolutely massive. I felt the rough texture of its white painted sides.

"That is one paint job I'd rather not repeat," said Finn.

Cat bent her head back and shaded her eyes. She peered all the way to the top. "You're kidding, right?" she said.

"Nope. Years ago I started up at the lantern room with a brush and paint bucket and did a little at a time. Took me the better part of a season, with breaks for weather of course.

Cat stood with her mouth open, finally forming words to say, "I'd be petrified."

"It still looks fresh," I said.

Finn nodded and grinned. "Glad to hear it. I'll let you in on a little secret. I keep touching up the bottom ten feet. I figure if that always looks sparkling, those in charge will think the whole tower looks good. They won't send me up to paint what they can't see."

He pulled open the heavy door, and we stepped into a small room at the bottom of the tower. My eyes immediately went to the thin, winding staircase.

"Go on," said Finn.

"Does it get narrower as we go?" Cat peered up the stairway. "I'm bigger than both of you. Will I get stuck halfway up?"

"Nobody's going to get stuck," said Finn with a chuckle. "After you, ladies."

I started up the stairs first with the others right below me. Without planning to, I found myself counting my steps.

"How many are there?" I was on step 79, and my legs were starting to wobble.

"196," said Finn.

Cat spoke between gasps of air. "Yikes, I'm never going to make it."

Finally, we reached the top. Whew. No wonder Finn was spry for his age, with all this stair climbing. Through the little windows we could gaze in every direction. The narrow island stretched beneath us like a long slab of green-apple Laffy Taffy.

"You can see more than ten miles out on a clear day." Finn pointed a gnarled finger towards the sea.

"One of those dots might be my dad's lobster boat," said Cat.

I watched a nearer sailboat pass by. It looked like a toy from this height.

"Here," said Finn, opening a door. "Let's try the gallery. Careful, now."

I followed him out to the balcony. A gust of wind slammed into me, leaving me plastered against the lighthouse wall. I hung onto the rail and took a few steps, making room for Cat to join us.

"Nuh huh, I'm staying in here," she said.

I inched around the top of the entire lighthouse, taking in the view as I went.

"Wow, that was fun!" I stepped back into the lantern room with Finn close behind me.

Finn chuckled. "Now you know how the outside of the windows get washed. Yep, and I'd come up here every night before sunset to light the lamp." Finn demonstrated the steps he took as he described them. "Then I'd pause to look out. Up and down the coast, lights would follow suit. Each one a sailor's lifeline. Quite a few storms, too. Always plenty to record in the logbook."

I looked up at the big light. "It must have been a lot of work."

"I still polish the brass and keep the lighthouse swept up. And sometimes, if there's a glitch, I have to turn on the light and air compressor in order to run the fog signal." Finn shook his head. "Of course now everything's got battery backups. Nothing like the old times. When I started here, there were no days off. I could climb these steps in my sleep. I'd keep the oil wicks lit from sunset to sunrise. I'd have to hand-wind a clockwork mechanism in the oil lamps to rotate them. And another thing I'd be handling was explosive fog signals."

"Yikes. You're lucky to still be here," I said.

Cat chewed her lip. "Can anything explode now?"

"Nope, we're safe," Finn said. "Back down we go. I'll show you a bit of the island before we eat."

My legs still felt wobbly. And going down all those stairs made my knees feel like they were going to crack into pieces. At the bottom, we stopped at Finn's place again. He gave us some grape Kool-Aid, pretzels, and a few minutes to catch our breath.

SOON FINN WAS ready to move on. "Now let me show you some of the haunts of this here island." I swore he had more energy than Cat and I put together.

Despite our sore muscles, we hiked for the good part of an hour. No matter where we went, the smacking of waves against the edges of the narrow island kept us on course. Finn showed us parts of an old shipwreck and hard grassy mounds that swelled up from the ground where he declared there were skulls buried. At one point we entered a tight grove of pine trees. A skinny dirt path coiled through them.

"After you, ladies," said Finn, as he directed us into the heart of the wood.

Cat's eyes got big. "It's kind of creepy. You go first, Amy."

I rolled my eyes and shoved a branch out of the way. "Sure. I'm not afraid."

From inside the grove, all sounds of the ocean became muffled, and the pine smelled wonderful. I heard the pleasant trill of a bird chirp now and again. Noting the strong sunlight a ways ahead of us, I judged us to be about halfway through, when a sudden loud rustle and snap to the left, made me jump.

"Eiiiiiiiii!" screamed Cat. She flung her arms around me.

I peered in through the trees and saw nothing. I released myself from Cat's grasp and turned to look at Finn. "What was that?"

Finn was doubled over in laughter. Finally he pulled himself together enough to say, "Gee whizzikers, I wish I had a camera!"

Cat pretended to scowl at him. "It's not *that* funny."

Finn gasped for breath. "If you could've seen the way the two of you jumped."

Still concerned, I glanced back to where the noise was. "But, what was it?"

"Watch and learn the oldest trick in the book." Finn held up a rock that had been concealed in his hand and then tossed it into the woods ahead of us. It rustled through the branches as it fell and then landed with a thud.

"Ah!" Cat jumped again, though with much less drama. "Stop!" she pleaded.

I joined Finn in his second round of laughter.

As we started along the trail again, we heard someone coming. A real person, unless the trees here knew how to whistle Yankee Doodle.

Three straggly looking kids with red hair came into view. The two little girls were almost identical, and their lanky older brother appeared to be about ten.

Finn exchanged some chitchat with them and then introduced us.

I felt self-conscious, as they inspected us.

Later, I asked, "Who were those kids? Where did they come from?"

"They live down the other end of the island. A whole parcel of them."

"There's more?"

"About five or six kids, last I counted."

"Where do they go to school?" said Cat.

"No traditional schooling for them. They learn as they go. Their parents teach them what they need to know. Guess they wanted their own little hippie commune. Darwin, the boy," Finn nodded in the direction they'd gone off in, "he's sharp as a tack. Always asking me questions about the lighthouse."

I kept thinking about those kids and how different their life must be from mine. No bullies in their world, I'd bet. A vision of Pamela, kicking my books down the center aisle of the school bus last year, flashed through my mind. Although, the island kids missed out on a lot of things, too, I decided. Like the library.

As we neared our starting point, delicious smells taunted our last steps.

"I'm famished." Cat licked her lips.

"Yep, let's eat up. I can't be getting you girls back late."

On another sheet of tarp, we sat on the little beach, each cradling a large plate of food in our laps. I discreetly blocked my nose and tried a tiny bite of clam. And then another. Not bad. The vegetables were full of flavor, the best I'd ever had.

Since I usually was not a big fan of seafood, the clambake went beyond all my expectations and then some. It was peaceful to eat by the water, and my legs welcomed the rest. I stretched them out past the tarp and wiggled my toes in the cool damp sand. I could have sat there watching the waves slap the shore forever. Regrettably, the sun lowered, and our day was done.

ON THE BOAT ride back, my mind filled with ideas. "Yes, we'll have an exhibit."

"Where?" said Cat.

"How about Tibbetts Hall?"

"Port Wells has a hall?"

"It's a big room in the basement of the Baptist church. They use it for town meetings, wedding receptions, whatever comes up."

"Ricky could make frames," said Cat. "He loves messing around with wood."

"Yes, that would be perfect!" I said with growing excitement. "Won't it be great, Finn?"

I wasn't sure he heard me over the roar of the motor, what with the boat's wake splashing all around him. I called out to him again, louder. "Good plan, Finn?"

Finally he said, "I suppose it might be good to clear some of those old canvases out of there. I mean if anybody wants them, I'm willin'."

So, it was decided.

"I'll talk to Mrs. Baldwin." I pursed my lips in the same way Mrs. Baldwin often did, and then nodded. "She'll know how to get use of the hall."

I turned around to see where we were headed. Strong blue-gray swells pulled us through the water. Beyond the surf, the distant shore—great dark rocks interrupted by little coves and beaches, and then our harbor—warm and welcoming. As land neared, the waves broke white against it, retreated smooth and calm, and then just as quickly, returned for another attack.

In preparation for my future writing goals, I made a mental note of all the sensory details. By the time we reached the pier, bright sun-splashed colors streaked across the sky. A lone duck's head bobbed in and out of the rippling waves. There would be lots to share in my diary that night. The end of a perfect day.

8

ON WEDNESDAY, I was a few minutes later than usual coming from my last class of the day. I hopped up the steps of the school bus just before the door squeezed shut. Then I stopped short. Huh? All through junior high, along with these first few weeks of high school, I'd always sat in the same seat—second from the front on the right. Usually Cat and I sat there together, except on Wednesdays, when she had her piano lessons. And now it was filled. With Claire. Luckily, she was by the window, studying her nails, and hadn't noticed me. I took a breath and swallowed. No way would I sit down next to her.

I glanced across the aisle to find an older kid hogging another double seat—his stuff spread out beside him. I moved past a few more rows. Never had I seen the bus this crowded. Suddenly, something was in the aisle and I tripped and flew forward. I clutched my books with one arm and threw my free hand out to grasp the back of one of the seats. I could feel my face burning, as I struggled to maintain my balance. A few more shaky steps, and finally, way at the back, I found an empty spot.

I perched on the edge of the seat to avoid bothering the person sitting by the window. When my pulse returned to normal, I surveyed the aisle ahead of me. Pamela was twisted around, smirking in my direction. She sat right about where I had fallen. Had she and Claire planned the seat mix-up, to force me to walk the length of the bus, so she could trip and humiliate me? I considered what Cat would do if this happened to her. Then, rather than look at Pamela, I became very interested in a Camaro traveling along beside us outside the bus window. The shiny red car stayed with us until we reached the turnoff for Port Wells. It worked a little, but inside I still felt sad. Why did they have to pick on me? Didn't they have anything better to do?

EARLIER IN THE week, I had spent a couple of fun hours over at the Fantinos' house, painting in letters on the new library sign. The three of us, Cat, Ricky, and I, had sprawled out on the kitchen linoleum, head to head, as we filled in the stenciled shapes with rich royal blue paint. Aside from a few painted elbows, we all decided we'd done a great job.

Now, from my station at the library desk, I looked out the door and saw Ricky arriving with the finished product. I ran outside to help him hang the new sign.

"Wow, this looks amazing!" I touched the silky clear coating Ricky had layered over our letters.

"That will protect it from the weather," said Ricky with satisfaction. "Here, can you hold it for a minute?"

"It's so professional." I took the large plaque with both hands. "Where did you learn to make stuff like this, anyway?"

"At school last year." Ricky kicked over an old lobster trap and then stood on it to mark off spots for the nails. "We had a really cool class called Machine Shop. The teacher was a carpenter, so we ended up learning more about woodworking than machines. Suited me fine."

"Oh, yeah, there used to be shop at our high school, too. They got rid of it a couple of years ago." I felt the smooth rounded corners of the sign, and my fingers burned to sand some wood. "One of Nancy's friends used to talk about all the cool things they did in shop. I wanted to take it so bad, but apparently there were no girls allowed. Girls could only take Home Economics."

Ricky nodded. "We had that class for the girls, too. Sewing and cooking, right?"

"Right. And we've still got that program. By the time I graduate I'll be a regular little Susie Homemaker." I rolled my eyes and tried to picture myself bustling around the kitchen in a ruffled apron. I handed the sign up to him, and a moment later it hung as though it had always been there. That's how perfect it looked.

We both stepped back to admire the entranceway. The glossy wood with dark blue lettering gave our building a whole new look. I ran up to the door and called through the screen.

"Come see the new sign, Mrs. Baldwin!"

She stumbled out, flustered at being interrupted. "What is it?" She followed our gaze up to the top of the door. "Mercy, mercy, what a lovely piece of work." She shook Ricky's hand. "We'll have to give you extra privileges at the library. As many books as you want for as long as you want with no fees incurred. This tiny library is really hitting the big time now."

We all laughed. Then Ricky went off to do his paper route, and I followed Mrs. Baldwin into the library to tackle a heap of fresh book donations. Two of the books were of great interest to me. An anonymous donor had left them outside in a paper bag, on the steps of the library. Both had copyrights of 1973, thus they were brand new. One was *The Princess Bride* and the other was *Summer of My German Soldier.* An added perk to working at the library was we got to read everything first. I stamped, processed, and checked them out to bring home with me.

CAT CAME BY at closing to see the new sign. "Looks super!" she said.

We wandered down towards the pier to extend our brief meeting. I told her a little bit about the bus episode, but I didn't make it a big deal, just mentioned how Claire was in my seat and how Pamela's foot got in the aisle.

"Are you okay?" said Cat with concern.

"I'm fine. You and Ricky always cheer me up."

"Am I seeing what I think I'm seeing?" said Cat, looking past me.

I looked from her surprised face to the shoreline. "Yes! It's Pup. It must be Pup. What other seal would come in so close?"

We started to race down to the beach until Cat stopped and continued on tiptoe. "I don't want to scare them away," she whispered. By then we could see the other seal Pup traveled with, further back.

I bent down, carefully placed my bag of books on a nearby rock and stretched my arms out. Cat was right behind me.

"Come here, Pup," I said. "Come meet Cat." Pup swam over and nuzzled my hands. At first he moved back when Cat reached out to pet him. "It's okay, Pup," I said.

Cat stretched her arm further and gently patted him. "Oh! He feels softer than I thought he would."

Pup twitched his long whiskers. His big round eyes never left us as he wiggled a little at the edge of the sand. He let out a squeaky bark.

Cat laughed. "I think he's trying to talk to us."

I pointed to the white patch of fur above his left eye. "No matter how big he gets, I'll always know Pup because of this little heart-shape."

"It is a heart! So cool!"

We each gave Pup one more hug before he turned and splashed his strong flippers back into the ocean. Then we watched the two seals swim out to deeper water.

Seeing Pup made me miss Craig. Did he ever think of us—me and Pup?

"I'm wicked glad I got to meet Pup," said Cat.

I grinned. "Me, too."

9

ON FRIDAY, WE got out of school early, so the teachers could have a meeting. The weather was as warm as midsummer. I went into the post office and Sally Johnson, nosiest post mistress this side of Texas, said, "Yoo hoo, you have mail!"

I couldn't believe she'd said, 'yoo hoo.' She sounded like her snotty daughter, Pamela. Mrs. Johnson held a postcard out to me, a few inches beyond my reach. I could tell by her twinkling eyes that not only had she read and memorized it, but had probably already reported its contents to half the county. My heart began to pound. I plucked the card from her fingers with a curt 'thank you' and tried my darnedest to pretend I had no interest in it, whatsoever. I thought my curiosity would burst by the time I reached the pier.

Finn had his easel over to one side of the dock. An old lobster boat was coming to life on his canvas. Still behind him, I peeked down at my card. There was a banner splashed across the front. It spelled Boston in big, block letters. Four photo squares of historic-looking buildings were beneath the sign. My fingers itched to flip it over, except, at that same moment, Finn turned around and greeted me, and I didn't want to snub him.

"Another great painting!" I said, coming up beside him.

Finn smiled. "It's getting there, but you're too easy. You think they're all great." Finn's smile faded. "I'm having second thoughts about the exhibit."

"Why?"

"Not sure my stuff is good enough. People are busy nowadays. They shouldn't waste their time.

"Nuh huh. We're not even going to discuss backing out." I gave his shoulder a playful nudge after he put his brush down on the edge of the easel. "Hey, I've worked hard on this. It's happening all right."

Finn jerked his thumb back to point out Al's General Store. "I was in there picking up a few odds and ends the other day, when a magazine cover at the cash register stopped me in my tracks. Andy Wyeth's latest painting was spread out in all its glory. Whoo-ee."

I rolled my eyes. "Nobody is expecting his work to be on display, and I guarantee your work is going to knock the socks off everyone who sees it."

With my curiosity ready to explode, I eventually removed myself to the end of the pier. I flipped over my postcard. It wasn't lengthy or the best penmanship—large and scrawling—but it was special to me. The postcard said:

Hi Amy, Told you I'd write. Boston is big and busy. What's new? C.

p.s. I'm still working on that song.

Back when summer was first dipping its toe in the water, I'd discovered Craig could play the guitar. He was really good. At least to my tone-deaf ears. I'd made a big deal out of his talent and when he told me he was leaving for Boston, he said he'd try to write something even better than a letter. A song. Just for me.

With my mail in my pocket, I had an extra little bounce in my step for the rest of the day. My only regret was that the goof forgot to put his return address on the card.

When I got home after a short shift at the library, I had to crawl over Nancy on the front steps. She was seated on her old oilcloth sit-upon that she'd made years before in Brownie Scouts. Under her chin was a big piece of foil-covered cardboard. With eyes closed, her head was tilted back to the sun gods.

I crept up close. "Boo!"

"Ah!" Nancy yelped and almost bounced out of her skin. "You, Brat!"

"One of these days, you're going to fry yourself permanently," I said.

"It's so nice out today. I'm trying to get enough of a tan to last me through the whole winter."

I laughed. "Wouldn't want to look like a plucked chicken like your little sister."

Once inside, I read my postcard one more time and then tucked it under my pillow. I left my window open a crack to coax in the last of summer. Then I immersed myself in *The Princess Bride* until it was way past my bedtime.

I WOKE ON Saturday to the *coo coo coo* of a mourning dove. Carried in on crisp breezes, its somber sound reminded me I had to fill in for Cat at the library.

"As you know," Mrs. Baldwin had said the day before. "Cat has an orthodontist appointment in the morning, and she might not be back in time. And story time is going wonderfully. We definitely should carry on with it, no matter what. I'd hate for the children to be disappointed. You can read them a story, Amy. *Right?* And perhaps a small craft?" She peered at me down her long nose. "Do you think you could do that?"

I had swallowed and then said, "Sure."

Now that it was Saturday morning, I made a point of getting to the library early to practice what I was going to read, beforehand. Unfortunately, the children were there even earlier. Four of them stared back at me from the corner story-time rug.

"Hi," I said. They all continued to stare while I organized the craft supplies. I figured we could make bookmarks after our story.

Finally one of the girls said, "Where's Cat?"

"She had an appointment."

And then another child joined in. "Where's Cat? Where's Cat?"

I grabbed *The Little Engine That Could* off the shelf and settled down to read. It was one of my old favorites, should be easy. I took a deep breath and started in.

A boy in a blue-striped shirt interrupted. "I already know that story."

"That's okay." I tried a warm smile. It didn't work. My mouth still felt like a straight, stressed line.

After I read three pages, one of the girls said, "Cat reads better. And she shows us the pictures."

"Where's Cat?" The same girl who had asked the question when I first arrived, now proceeded to shout it over and over. "Where's Cat? Where's Cat? Where's Cat?"

I glanced towards the only child who I thought might be enjoying the story. A tear slid down her cheek.

"Okay, then." I tried to act confident and cheerful. "Let's move on to crafts!" Either nobody heard me or nobody cared. The turmoil continued.

I was ready to give up when I saw all four faces brighten. I turned around and there was Cat, her hands full of lollypops.

"Hi, kids, everyone having a good time?" she asked in her hearty, fun-loving voice.

"Yay, Cat's back!" the children screamed, in turn. They jumped up to hug Cat, yank on her braid, and get as close to her as they could, until they nearly toppled her over.

I could only sit like a miserable heap, but I was smiling as much as the kids. We were all elated to have Cat back.

After the kids left, I told Cat about my postcard.

She jumped up and gave me a big squeeze. "Oh, Amy, it's *so* romantic!" Cat sighed with her hands crossed at her chest. "You've got to show me ASAP. But not tonight. I'll be going back to Portland with my parents for a play at our old church."

"Have fun!" I said as we said our goodbyes. And I truly meant it, for as much as I loved spending time with Cat, I was kind of glad to have an empty night ahead. I couldn't wait to find out what would happen to Buttercup next in *The Princess Bride.*

HOWEVER, THINGS DON'T always go as planned. Around eight that night, Nancy started hollering about something that sounded like smoke.

Nancy's bedroom window looked out the front of the house and despite all the pine trees, she had a pretty good view over the top of them. "Fire! Down by the pier!"

10

I THREW DOWN my book, raced across the hall, and bolted to the window before she could yell at me to get out of her room. Distant gray smoke curled into the sky. My stomach churned as a chill raced up my back. No. It couldn't be the library! Not Miss Cogshell's special home, not after all I'd done to save it. I grabbed my flashlight, raced down the stairs past my mother on her way up, and flew out the door. The siren of a fire engine screamed across the dusky port, while I practically rolled down the hill.

As I got closer, I realized it wasn't the library. I paused and thanked the heavens for this miracle. The smoke was coming from *behind* the library. It must be the woodshed. Yikes, that could be even worse. My first thoughts were with Finn. Was he safe? Or had he already settled down in there for the night? I picked up my pace again and bolted around to the back of the library.

"Keep back," yelled a fireman when I tried to get closer to the burning woodshed. Great billows of smoke circled above the smoldering flames. The shack itself was nearly demolished and ashes were piled high. Where was Finn?

I let my flashlight flicker over the edges of the backyard. Finally its glow landed on a slumped figure near the pine trees on the far side of the lawn. I ran over. Finn sat with all his equipment heaped around him.

"Finn! Are you okay?" I dropped down beside him. "What happened?" I gasped for breath in the smoky air.

"I'm fine." He coughed. "Can't say the same for your air mattress though."

"Don't worry about that old junk. Were you still inside?"

"Yep. I was just warming up a can of beans on the old woodstove, when I heard voices. I shoved open the door and two young-ums about your age skedaddled away. They'd been sitting alongside the wall of the shed there." Finn attempted a chuckle and then coughed again. "Never in their lives did they expect the likes of me to come outta that there woodshed." Finn glanced around. "There they are. Over there." He pointed to a group of people watching the firefighters work. To one side stood Pamela and Claire. Pamela had her arms crossed like she watched destruction every day of her

71

life and Claire looked bored, too, twirling a strand of hair round and round her finger.

"A bit later I smelled smoke and took a look around," Finn continued. "By the time I circled the whole outside of the shed, there were flames busting out all over. I grabbed my stuff and got the heck out of there."

I swallowed and took a minute to think about what might have happened. After another moment's hesitation, I carefully asked, "What did you do with the match you used to light the stove?"

"Threw it right in like I always do." He looked at me. "Amy, you don't think I caused the fire, do you?"

"No, of course not." It took a moment to slow my breathing. Beams of light circled as firemen continued to spray the last of the flames. The heavy ashy smell filled the air stronger now. We moved back a few feet as I continued to puzzle out the events. "How did the fire engine get here so quickly?"

"The postmistress over there." Finn pointed out Sally Johnson. "She called from the post office. She was popping in to get something and was about to lock up again, she said, when she smelled smoke."

While we were talking, I noticed that Pamela and Claire had inched closer to us. Suddenly Pamela yelled out, "There's the man who started the fire!" She spun around, as though looking for whoever would care. "We saw him running out of the woodshed."

Howard the harbormaster walked over to her.

"There!" she said pointing at Finn.

"And where were you when you saw him?" asked Howard.

"Me and Claire were over by the pier, and we smelled something smoky."

Claire nodded her head in agreement. My mouth fell open. Hadn't Finn said they were next to the shed? Could they really have made it to the pier before they smelled anything?

Howard motioned for Finn to come over, and the two of them walked around to the front of the library to talk for a while.

Later, Finn came back and stood quietly beside me. From a grove of pine trees, we watched the fire dwindle and give up its fight against the blasts of water. I picked out Nancy and Mom in the group of people who watched by the edge of the road. Nothing like a fire to pull everyone away from what they were doing.

"Will everything be okay?" I asked.

"Howie's just doing his job. It will all work out." Finn's troubled eyes didn't look as certain as his words.

An odd shout rang out. Finn looked at me.

I shrugged my shoulders and listened. "Did that sound like my name to you?"

Another hoarse shout: "Amy!"

Who would be calling me? I wondered. My father? Maybe. Although the voice sounded too high and frantic for Dad and as far as I knew, he was still tied up with work. I stepped out of the trees. "Here!"

Ricky rushed up to me. "Thank goodness." He reached his arms out almost as though he was going to hug me, but then pulled them back quick to hang by his sides.

"What? What is it?"

"I biked home from across town." He paused to catch his breath. "The rest of my family is in Portland."

"Yes?"

"So much smoke. I thought it was the library." Ricky looked down and said softly, "I know how important that building is to you and I needed to know you were okay."

I was surprised he understood about the library. Or was he just saying that? How could anyone besides Craig know how special Miss Cogshell's house was to me? Nevertheless, Ricky was right. This whole night could have been much worse. Even Ricky's new library sign might have perished in the fire.

I felt the heat of my face rise to match the burning embers. "Yeah, I'm fine."

Right then, my father did show up. I filled him in on all that had taken place.

"What about Finn?" I looked out towards the water. "He can't take the boat home. He never carries any kind of lantern, and it's way too dark out there."

Dad went over and shook hands with Finn and then asked, "Say, do you need a place to stay tonight?"

"Oh, I'll be all right." Finn began to lift up his pile of art supplies.

From behind Finn, I nodded my head fiercely in support of my father's idea. I sure hoped Finn wouldn't do anything foolish.

"Well, all the same," said my father. "We've got one of those new sleep sofas. Why don't you come back with us?" And so it was decided.

BETWEEN THE FOUR of us, we made light work of getting Finn and his stuff up the hill towards home.

"Say hi to Cat for me when she gets back," I said to Ricky before he left. What a night. I had tons to tell her.

"That was some fire." Nancy emerged from her room. She stopped short when she entered the living room.

"Yes and everyone is safe," said Dad. He and Finn each pulled at either end of the sleep sofa as they tried to release the mattress.

"Thank goodness for that," said Mom. "I'll go get sheets and then I'll heat up some of those doughnuts we fried earlier."

Nancy still stared. She looked at me and mouthed, "Who is that?"

I motioned her back into the hallway. "That's Finn. He'll be staying here."

"Here? In our house? Isn't that kind of creepy?" She sniffed. "The whole house smells like smoke now."

"That's what fires do," I said.

Nancy darted another glance through the doorway. "Is he homeless?" she whispered loudly.

I explained about the lighthouse and woodshed and tried to make it all appear normal.

Nancy shook her head. "Well, I guess it's good he'll have a place to sleep. One night. Still, I'll be shoving my nightstand up against the door."

"Well, let me introduce you first." I steered Nancy into the room, feeling as though I had become the big sister.

She and Finn exchanged a brief hello. Between his flushed face and sloppy appearance, he didn't appear any more comfortable than Nancy at being introduced. But I was pleased that she politely said good night to him before she went off to the safety of her room.

After enjoying a warm cinnamon doughnut, I, too, finally got ready for bed. My head buzzed with the day's events. Tonight, *The Princess Bride* would have to wait. Feeling a little like John Boy Walton, from the TV show, I filled six pages of my diary. I took more care with penmanship and sentence structure now, because you never could tell, future stories might someday come from these words.

11

THE FOLLOWING THURSDAY, Ricky came in right before closing. He carried a large flat bag. "You said you couldn't wait to see the frames I'm making, so I brought a few over."

"Oh, great!" I got up to get a better look. "These are amazing. This weather-beaten wood will be perfect for the ocean scenes."

"Some of that came from leftover woodshed strips. I've made almost thirty of them." Ricky proudly held up another frame. "Took some measuring—this one is sixteen by twenty. I'll put little nails here and there to hold the canvas in."

"These will really set off Finn's work," I said.

After the one night at our house, Finn had resumed boating back and forth from the island; although some days he didn't come at all. He said he was working on a few small projects that didn't rely as much on having long stretches of daylight. Because whether we were ready or not, the days grew shorter, and the leaves were starting to show their bright fall colors.

I watched Ricky point out the details of his frames, in his musical voice. This made it all real—like the exhibit would truly happen now, thanks to Ricky. "Wow. I can't believe how many you've made."

Ricky's face glowed, almost like he'd done all this to win my praise—fat chance, although it still made me feel less shy.

"I really appreciate all the times you've helped out," I told him. "You're always doing thoughtful things for the library and now with the exhibit, too."

Ricky flushed and gave me a big smile, his chipped tooth showing. He was so cute. And sweet, in a nerdy way.

I smiled back. Then I turned away and did a quick check to make sure the library windows were all closed.

Ricky followed close behind. "Uh, Amy, I was wondering something."

"What?" I said distractedly. I stuffed homework into my notebook, grabbed my jacket, and prepared to leave. Then I looked back at Ricky. Why wasn't he speaking? Oh, my gosh. He looked like those guys in the old movies Nancy liked to watch. They always got a weird look on their faces before they said something mushy. Embarrassed, I got busy again, stupidly re-checking the windows until the moment had passed.

"Forget it." Ricky slipped the frames back into his bag. He looked relieved and disappointed all at once, but soon cheered up. "Hey, can I get you a frappe at Al's?"

"Oh." I looked at my watch. Drat, almost dinner time, but I did love those extra-thick milkshakes. "Uh, sure. We could stop by."

All day long during school, I'd been anxious to get home and read my book. After finishing *The Princess Bride,* I was halfway through *Summer of My German Soldier.* Both books were amazing, and I couldn't imagine ever being able to write as well as William Goldman or Bette Greene. They transported me to faraway places. What a bookworm I'd turned into. The memory of Pamela's name-calling flashed through me, but I dashed it away. She wasn't going to ruin my day. And on this day, my reading would have to wait. Frappes and boys were important, too.

I locked up the library, and we walked over to Al's General Store. The four shiny stools lined up at the soda fountain were empty. After a moment of 'I don't care, where do you want to sit?' we chose the two middle seats. Ricky placed his bulky package of frames on top of the stool beside him. I nervously spun my seat round and round, until I felt dizzy.

Al tied a white apron around his stout middle, as he moved from the front cash register, back to the food area. "What can I get you two?"

"What would you like, Amy?" said Ricky.

Never good at food decisions, I shrugged. "What are you going to have?"

"A strawberry frappe."

"I'll have that, too."

Soon we both had huge frothy pink drinks in front of us. They were so thick I had to use my spoon more than my straw, and I knew already I'd have no room for dinner.

Ricky tossed a few quarters on the counter.

"I'll pay you back tomorrow," I said.

"Nope, my treat."

"Are you sure?"

"Yep." He grinned. "I've got to spend my paper route money on something."

Ricky walked me partway home until he agreed with me that the frames were getting too heavy to lug much further.

"Well, thanks," I said. "That was fun."

"Yeah, it was like a date," said Ricky.

"Wow, I'd never believe I'd go on a date."

"Why not?"

"Well, ya know, because I'm shy," I said.

"You're shy?"

"Definitely," I said. "You should have seen me last year before. . ." my voice trailed off. "I mean, I couldn't even give an oral report. Ha, and you should see me trying to do Cat's story time. I guess I just make myself do things, though, even if I'm shaking in my boots."

We both laughed and said goodbye one more time. How funny, I thought. Ricky didn't think I was shy. Maybe other people couldn't even tell when somebody got that overwhelming, shaking hot fear inside. And now look at me: I'd actually been on a date.

Trudging the last steps to home, I realized I'd had a lot of fun lately, and hadn't been thinking as much about Craig. Like, not at all.

THE FOLLOWING DAY, I was happy to discover Finn back on the pier. "Wanted to get one last island sketch in before my hand freezes up."

"Is it working out okay, now that you're not staying overnight?"

"Yep, I'm just about done for the season anyway."

I inhaled deeply the sweet, fresh breath of the sea. "Yeah, it's getting cold all right," I agreed. "I can't wait for the exhibit, though. Ricky's made about thirty frames, so we should be all set. Wait until you see them, they're perfect." I took a little card out of my back pocket and handed it to Finn. It was the announcement with times and dates included.

"Whoo-ee, is this really being spread all over town?" For a minute, Finn looked like a frightened, little boy as he studied one of the promo cards Cat and I had made. He rubbed his hands together and then picked up his brush again. "I better finish this thing and start sorting through my stuff."

I studied his latest work. "Don't you worry. Everyone's going to love your paintings." I zipped my jacket against the windless chill and got ready to make my exit.

I stopped in my tracks as a car pulled up. "Isn't that the county sheriff's car?"

Finn lifted his eyes from his picture and his face darkened. We watched a huge man dressed in uniform, emerge from the car.

"Howdy, folks." He tipped his hat, a hat that reminded me of the park ranger's in Yogi Bear cartoons. "Might you be Mr. Finn Eriksson?"

Finn nodded.

"I have a summons-to-court date for you." The large man handed Finn an official looking envelope. "Still a ways off, but there you have it."

"What for?" I blurted.

The Sheriff looked at Finn.

"Yeah, Amy, I've been meaning to tell you about that," Finn said. "Looks like I got me arrested for trespassing, vandalism, and maybe even arson."

My jaw dropped. This couldn't be happening. Why, even I had gone into the woodshed now and again, to get a tool or whatever.

After the Sheriff left, I said, "You can't go to jail, right? I mean, you didn't do anything wrong."

Finn gave a sad grin. "Could be just a fine."

I thought of his modest dwelling at the lighthouse and his meager belongings. He didn't have money to spare on fines. "It's not fair."

"I suppose it is—I had no right to be there."

"Sure you did. Nobody owned the woodshed, and you're bringing beauty to the world."

As the sun dropped lower and the tide rose higher, Finn climbed into his boat and we went our separate ways, all thoughts of exhibits pushed from my mind. No way was he an arsonist. Even if Finn *had* caused the fire, he hadn't done it on purpose.

As soon as I got home, I went to the closed door of my father's office. He usually had a lot of paperwork to do and didn't like to be disturbed. I put my ear to the door. Well, at least he wasn't on the phone. I gave a quick double rap and entered, after he acknowledged the interruption. I think he could tell by my face that it was important. He put down his pen.

"What is it Amy?"

"Finn's being blamed for the fire."

"How do you know this?"

"He got a sums."

"A summons?"

I nodded.

"I'm sorry to hear that." Dad frowned and scratched his head. "Well, if he can't afford his own, they'll give him a court-appointed lawyer. If he's innocent, it should all work out in his favor."

"What do you mean? Of course, he's innocent!"

"I'm sure it will work out fine, then. Probably only one brief session. When does he go?"

I told him the date, but something niggled at my mind as I closed the door behind me. Did my father really feel there was any question of Finn's innocence? Whether Finn *had* dropped his match and set the woodshed on fire, what would happen then?

I called Cat on the phone that night and we tried to figure it all out, deciding, in the end, that we would most certainly be at that trial.

12

NOW THAT WE were into October, the days grew colder and the nights longer. One day, Cat came up behind me in the school hallway where I was reading a poster about the Harvest Dance. She rested her square chin on my shoulder and peered at the bulletin board. "Ya know, anybody can go to this dance," she said.

With a laugh, I shook her off.

"We could even go together," she continued. "Why should we miss out just because Pamela says everyone should have a date?"

Cat's voice carried.

"Shh." I glanced down the corridor. "Wouldn't we look stupid?"

Cat spun around to stare into my face, her thick braid nearly swatting me in the eye. "Won't *we* look stupid? Why would we look any more stupid than the rest of them? I mean come on. We're probably the smartest in our class."

"I don't mean that."

"What? You don't think we look cool enough? Gee whiz, Amy." Cat made a face and went into her classroom.

I was worried I'd hurt her. Gosh, she looked fine. It was only me, with my stringy hair and string bean body to match.

THAT AFTERNOON, MRS. Baldwin came into the library a bit late. "Had to pick up our mail and once me and Sally get jabbering, time flies." She flipped through a small stack of envelopes. "Oh, my. This isn't for the library."

I looked up from the forty-year-old book I was repairing—a well-read copy of *Ben of Old Monhegan*. The binding had fallen apart and needed strong glue along the gutter to seal it back together. "Who's it for?" I asked.

She handed me the envelope, and as soon as I saw the airmail stamps going across the outside, I got a funny feeling in my stomach. In black ink, neat cursive lines spelled *Miss Sylvia Cogshell*. I swallowed. "What should we do?"

Mrs. Baldwin frowned. "Apparently it's from someone who didn't know she'd passed on."

I nodded.

"Well, I suppose we could jot 'deceased' on the front and send it back," she said.

How horrible, I thought. "It's her pen pal from England. Miss Cogshell told me about her. They were in college together."

Mrs. Baldwin attempted to take back the letter. I didn't loosen my grip. "I'll take care of it," I said, giving the envelope a final yank.

I supposed I had two options. Either write a few lines and then put both items into a bigger envelope or rip into the letter and learn more about Miss Cogshell's friend. And then, of course, send a letter back. I definitely found the second plan more tempting. In fact I couldn't wait to get inside the envelope. I rationalized it by telling myself it would be nice to at least address her by name. Her return label only stated her location on a road in Sheffield. I placed the letter on the desk in front of me and waited.

When Mrs. Baldwin was finally busy shelving books in a far corner of the back room, I had my chance. Before I slipped my finger all the way into the envelope to carefully unfasten the seal, I stopped. It didn't seem right. It's not like it was one of Nancy's silly letters she always left lying around. It belonged to the person I had respected most—Miss Cogshell. I sighed and flipped the letter back upside down to deal with later.

That's when I realized the seal was nearly unstuck. It must have been loose to begin with and then became unattached when we had our little tug-a-war. I shook my head with a smile. What's meant to be is meant to be.

Dear Sylvia, I haven't heard from you in quite some time.... It was a cool letter, filled with newsy events; however the paragraph that caught my eye most said the following: *Sylv, I'm very pleased to learn of your new friends and how much joy they have brought you. Amy and Craig must be remarkable young people. And Pup! How fun to hear of his adventures.*

Her friend signed her name as Margie. That's right, Miss Cogshell had often spoken of Margie. Not knowing for sure if it was short for Margaret, I would have to use it as is.

AN HOUR LATER, Ricky found me still sitting there, the tears in my eyes now dry. I had poured out my heart on a piece of scrap paper and would transfer it to my best stationery when I got home.

Dear Margie,
(I hope it's okay to address you informally, but I have no other name to use.) I am so sad to have to tell you some very bad

news. Miss Cogshell passed away at the end of June. She had a stroke but did not suffer. I'm very sorry. I know you were good friends. I hope you don't mind that I read your personal letter to her, but I did. It was delivered to us here at the library because her home has become the Port Wells Public Library. Although for only a short time, she was a very special friend to me, too. Also to Craig, who I hope will come home soon so I can tell him about your letter, as well as everything else he is missing out on. He's in Boston, but should be back one of these days. Oh, and you mentioned Pup in your letter! I have seen him several times down at the pier. He has a friend.

Miss Cogshell told me a bunch of funny stories about when the two of you were in college together. I have recently considered a writing career for myself and wondered if you would mind if maybe we could be pen pals now, you know, for practice, and because you seem like a very nice lady. I don't usually talk very much. Somehow it feels easier to send my words across the sea to you.

Sincerely,

Amy Henderson

"So," Ricky said about ten times, more nervous than usual.

I put Margie's letter plus my reply to her into the pocket of my notebook.

"So, what?"

"I guess you've heard about the dance," he finally spit out with a rush of air.

"Yeah. . ."

"Wanna go?"

"Well, I think your sister wants to, but I'm not sure."

Now he was really blushing. "No, I mean you and me."

I caught his eye quick before he could turn away. "You mean like. . .?"

"Yes, like a date."

Wow. Wouldn't that be something? Me walking in with the cute new boy. Well, I did realize a few certain people might think he was a goober, because he was smart and studious looking, ... Hmm, he might be the one person in the school who didn't think *I* looked like a freak. On the other hand, was it fair to Ricky when, until recently, all I seemed to think about was Craig? I was so immersed in my thoughts that Ricky must have misunderstood.

"Don't answer yet. I don't need to know for a few weeks." With a disappointed face, he hurried out of the library.

I TOSSED AND turned all night. Of course, I should say yes to my very first dance invitation; or should I? I mean some girls waited until they were at least eighteen to date and that had always seemed like a fine plan to me. Even Nancy didn't go out on a real date until the day after her sixteenth birthday. And ever since she'd been piling up the broken hearts. I could still remember that first poor kid who used to call every night after she'd invited him to the Twist Twirl years ago. The minute she could date, he took her out about ten times. Then she decided he was too dull. He was a senior, and now that I was in the same school I sometimes saw him between classes in the corridor. We never acknowledged each other, though. I was too afraid to look him in the eyes. Afraid I'd still see that kicked puppy dog look.

13

THE NEXT DAY, I stood on the pier and looked out over the water. It was a daily habit to check for my favorite little seal. No Pup today. And with temperatures dipping into the forties—no sign of Finn either. I missed watching him work and hoped he wasn't getting too worried about his court appearance.

I glanced back towards the library and wondered if Ricky would be down here again today. Trying to make up my mind about the dance was driving me crazy. It would be cool to walk in with Ricky, except would my parents even let me go on a real date? And what about Cat?

A whistle made me turn towards the little beach.

A boy with long, blonde hair, sat cross-legged on the sand. He almost blended in with the heap of driftwood and old lobster traps beside him, but his grin shined through it all. "'Bout time you showed up," he called out.

My body started shaking before my mind even realized what was going on. Craig! Could he really be back? I rushed over and stopped short. I mean, really. Just because we hugged once, it didn't mean I could hurl myself at him again. That old shyness came creeping back. I glanced down at the sand. "Hi."

"Hi, yourself. Did you miss me?"

I nodded and smiled. An understatement if I'd ever heard one.

"What's been going on around here?" Craig shoved back his hair and grinned up at me again.

I laughed. It was so good to see him. How could I even begin to share all he'd missed? "How've *you* been?" I said instead. "And, hey, where's your old army jacket?"

Craig shrugged. He used to wear a beat-up green military coat every single day. Now he wore a heavy blue sweatshirt. It matched his eyes and, of course, looked great on him.

"I guess it died of old age," he said. "Back in Boston."

We both laughed. Last August, Craig's mom had gone to a treatment center. She had a drinking problem. There wasn't room for Craig to stay at his Portland aunt's place with the rest of his siblings, so he had gone down to Massachusetts to be with another aunt for a couple of months. Lately, until this moment when

I actually laid eyes on him, I hadn't let myself believe he'd ever come back.

"I got your postcard." I felt a blush rising as I pictured it smooshed beneath my pillow.

"Hey, a promise is a promise."

"Did you wri. . ..I mean, are you really going to. . .."

"Of course, I'm writing you a song. I've got it half done." He continued to sit while I stood fidgeting with the hem of my jacket. Even though only a couple of months had gone by, Craig looked older now.

However, he still seemed to know what I was going to say before I said it, like we'd never been apart. He scooped up handfuls of sand and let them spill as though through a funnel back onto the beach. "Hard to find this in the city."

"So much has happened." I bounced up and down on my heels a couple of times. "We're going to sell Finn's paintings. Cat and I thought of it on the island." I suddenly couldn't stop babbling. "And then there's the trial. We can't let him go to jail because of the fire."

Craig stood up and reached out to steady me. "Whoa, slow down. Fire? Jail? A cat on the island? And who the heck is Finn?"

"The fire was in the woodshed," I said. "Behind the library. I mean, behind Miss Cogshell's." I felt my lip tremble. Only Craig would truly understand what a tragedy it would have been to lose Miss Cogshell's house. "It was horrible. I thought—"

"You thought it was her house at first?"

I nodded.

"Aw, that must have stunk." Craig reached out and touched my shoulder. He glanced over at the library. "Nope. Can't ever lose Miss C's place. Too bad about the woodshed though. I really dug that spot. Just smelling it, made me want to pick up a hammer and saw and build something."

I nodded with appreciation.

Craig laughed. "Ha, that would be a first. A regular old woodworker I'd be."

I thought of how much Ricky liked to work with wood. I was about to answer the rest of Craig's questions when I realized he was looking past me. One eyebrow arched, as his grin faded.

I turned to find Ricky coming up fast behind me. I couldn't read his face. "Amy?" He shot a dark scowl at Craig and then looked back at me. "Are you okay, Amy?"

I couldn't speak or even swallow. How strange to see them here, both at once. I formed the necessary words. "I'm fine. Ricky, this is Craig. Craig, Ricky."

Craig nodded.

Ricky didn't budge at first. Then he relaxed his expression and appeared a little more receptive. It would be great if my two friends liked each other, could maybe even hang out together.

"This is Cat's brother," I said to break the silence.

"Ah," said Craig. "Are you a cat, too, or do they call you Dog?"

Ricky stuck his lip out. He looked small and shy next to Craig. And even though Ricky was older, he didn't look as old as Craig.

"Cat is short for Caterina," I said. "They moved here a few months ago."

Ricky and Craig eyed each other warily.

"They're my friends," I added.

Ricky, still dumbstruck, looked self-conscious.

"Cool," said Craig. "Well. You *have* been busy."

The three of us stood in uncomfortable silence for a minute until I bent down to tie the shoelace of my sneaker. Anything to break up the awkwardness.

Then Craig spoke again. "I've got a bunch of stuff to do, so I've got to split. We'll catch up later." He smiled at me, kind of a half-smile, and then shot a last glance at Ricky before he left.

"I guess Craig will be back in school tomorrow," I said.

Ricky let out a sigh. "Who is that guy anyway?"

I tried to fill him in as best I could. "Well, ya know, when we found the wounded seal pup, that's when Craig and I became friends," I explained.

Ricky seemed a little jealous. "I like seals," he said with a shrug.

I stayed down at the pier for longer than usual, to make up for not having made a decision about the dance yet. The entire time, a small elated voice in my head sang, *'Craig's back, Craig's back!'*

ON THURSDAY, WITHIN minutes, the whole school knew that Craig had returned. After all the rumors about where he'd been had circulated, I was surprised and relieved that most of the kids still thought he was cool and that his mother's problems hadn't changed anything. There was a circle around him at all times while he told of his Boston adventures. Apparently, he'd spent a lot of his stay hanging out with an older cousin.

"You went to a what?" asked one of the guys, a track star I'd never met, but had certainly heard about.

"A disco," said Craig. "It's a new kind of dance club. Big in New York, too. On Sunday afternoons they let underage kids in." He grinned at his audience and pretended to lower his voice. "Plus, I snuck in a couple times using my cousin's ID."

"I thought the drinking age was 21 there," said one of the girls.

"Nope, they reduced it to eighteen a few months back, and since I'm such a big guy, I got in, no sweat."

The track star laughed and said, "Did you get plastered?"

"Nah," said Craig. "Too busy grooving to the tunes."

I let out the breath I hadn't realized I'd been holding. It would crush me if Craig followed in his mother's footsteps. He was way too special to waste his life on alcohol.

I looked up and down the hallway and wondered where Cat was. We always met at her locker before English class, so we could walk in together.

From a safe distance I continued to watch Craig. My stomach churned when I saw him check out a couple of those newly grown-up-looking girls who walked by on platform shoes. The hall was getting overly crowded. I looked away when I saw one of Nancy's rejected dates amble by.

And then I saw Cat coming. Her face looked flushed. Had she been running? No, on second glance she didn't seem to be in any hurry. She turned to look up at the boy beside her. Ah, they were walking together. He was tall and skinny and had curly red hair. When they finally reached me, he said, "See you later!"

I looked after him and then turned back to Cat. "Who was that?"

She lowered her eyes. "That's Jeremy. We're in Science together."

"Inter-r-esting," I said. Cat gave me a swat, and we moved on to our classroom.

14

TWO DAYS LATER I sat in the library and tried to figure out what to do about the dance. If only Miss Cogshell was still alive for me to confide in. Should I go with Ricky? Was I ready to go on a *real* date? Did Cat even know he'd asked me?

And then who should walk through the door, but Craig. Immediately, my knees got wobbly. What was it about him?

Craig looked around the library and gave a salute when he saw Clyde, Miss Cogshell's old walking stick with the turtle head. Her novelty cane now hung over the reptile section of books. Then he stopped in front of me.

"Hey, Sunshine. I was thinking we should hit the dance together." Craig shoved his blonde hair up out of his eyes. "Ya know, as a way to make up for that bizarre Twist Twirl last year."

Sunshine? And since when was the Twist Twirl *bizarre?* Was that yet another Boston word? The Twist Twirl had been the eighth grade dance. It was set up so the girls got to invite the boys. I tried like anything to get up the nerve to ask Craig, but instead he ended up going with Pamela. Luckily, Pamela had a new crush this year.

I could barely think straight. "Are you asking me out?"

"Duh, yeah." Craig laughed, his shiny white teeth sparkling. All thoughts of Ricky's invitation flew from my mind. I didn't get it. Craig was incredibly popular. Why in the world would he want to go with me? Was he so beyond worrying about his looks that he didn't notice or care how others looked? So certain of his class standing, as Nancy would say, that he knew nothing could shake it? Or did he not bother with that sort of stuff? Too many questions.

Instead, I said, "You seem a little different since your visit to Boston." Craig acted much older now. More like he should be hanging out with Nancy's crowd. Of course he was still a great guy, except a *guy,* not a kid. The way our birthdays were, we were almost a year apart anyway, and I'd be the first to admit I was young for my age. Sometimes, I'd overhear other girls talking about stuff on the bus, and I'd feel like they were more grown up than me, especially in the going out with boys department.

"Nah, same old me." He tossed a paperback book up over his head and caught it behind his back. No wonder I was shy of him. He was even more confident now, almost cocky. But then he looked at me, and I saw my old friend behind those blue eyes.

"Amy, they're way ahead of us down there. Stores are everywhere, restaurants, too. At one of the places we'd hang out, they had this cool arcade game called Pong. And all the latest movies are showing. They've got a new guy playing James Bond."

"Oh, yeah," I said. "I like that "Live and Let Die" song."

"And you should see the New England Aquarium. I got talking to one of the seal trainers. I guess there's this guy up here in Rockport, Maine, who raised a pet seal. He calls him André. He's gonna have him board at the aquarium in Boston for the winter. Then he'll be released into the ocean by summer. He figures if he wants to come home, he'll find his way, even though it's almost a 200 mile swim."

"Wow. He thinks seals can go all that way on their own?"

"Yep. The trainer seemed to think he could do it, too."

"That's amazing. I always *thought* our seal friend was smarter than he looked."

We both laughed, remembering Pup.

"Seeing the aquarium seals and hearing about André made me wish we still had Pup." Craig brushed his hair back, began fiddling with a stack of books, and then shifted from one foot to the other as he bent to peer through the little window towards the road. I could tell he was trying to stay focused, but was already out there in that ocean air.

The whole time we were talking about seals, the words *sunshine dance sunshine dance sunshine dance* bounced through my mind. I couldn't believe my dream from last spring had come true—that Craig had asked me to go to the dance with him. I squirmed under his gaze and knew he was still waiting for my answer. I started to give a jumbled reply when, at the same moment, a customer with a question came in and slammed the door. With relief I turned my attention to the portly woman looking for cookbooks. I kept thinking about Craig's invitation, wondering how I should answer.

Of course I would give anything to go to a dance with Craig, but Ricky asked me first and that should count for something. Besides, I liked Ricky, too. Was I really that messed up?

It took a while to find the right recipe collection for my customer. Out of the corner of my eye I saw Craig motion to me. "Think about it," he mouthed. Then off he went. Whew, more time for me to decide.

BY THE TIME Mrs. Baldwin came in, my mind was like a tangled fishnet. I decided to ask her about it, in a roundabout way of course.

"Mrs. Baldwin," I said. "What would you do if you had two dates to the same dance?"

"Oh, that's easy," she said crisply. "I'd go with who-ever I liked best and tell the other fellow, 'No, thank you'."

I thought about how Craig seemed changed, almost too old for me, and how comfortable I'd become with Ricky. "But, whether you liked both of them best in different ways?"

Mrs. Baldwin fiddled with a few of the card catalog drawers. Being a discarded piece of equipment sent over from the Thomaston library, none of the boxes fit smoothly and, therefore, needed frequent adjustment. With a frustrated sigh and a last thump on the crooked drawer, she finally answered me. "Who makes your heart flutter and skip a beat?" She bent down to grab her purse. "You'll figure it out. I've got to run over to Al's for a box of paperclips. You're in charge." And off she went.

I tried to focus on my heart. Feeling like an idiot, I closed my eyes and let Craig's name repeat over and over in my head while I concentrated on beats and possible flutters. Then I did the same thing with Ricky's name. After giving them each about two minutes, I snapped my eyes open. "This is ridiculous," I muttered. I couldn't even keep track of my heartbeats, never mind knowing if they fluttered or not. I sighed. A lot of help Mrs. Baldwin was.

Next, I picked up a small square of paper and pretended it was a daisy full of petals. He loves me, he loves me not. I ripped the paper into smaller and smaller pieces. I did it with both names and four different squares of paper. Craig's turn came out as 'he loves me' the first time, and 'he loves me not' the second time. Ricky's? The same. Argghh! Maybe I was tearing the paper smaller one time than the other? Who knows? Obviously it was a poor way to make a decision.

I'd have to ask Cat if she had one of those fortune-telling Magic 8 balls. Since Ricky was her brother and she didn't have even one invitation to the dance, I didn't want to come right out and ask her what I should do.

The last thing she needed to hear was that I had a second invitation.

I don't know how long I sat there, but before I knew it, Mrs. Baldwin was back from the store. She paused to frown at the floor around my chair. "Where in the world did all this confetti come from?" she asked.

"Oh!" I jumped up and collected my silly love scraps.

As I was leaving, Cat came in to do her shift. "Cat, do you have an Eight Ball?"

"Nope. What do you want one for?"

"I'm trying to make a decision."

"About the dance?"

I nodded.

"Let me guess. Craig asked you to go with him."

My eyebrows shot up. "How did you know?"

Cat rolled her eyes. "Come over on Saturday. I have something better than an Eight Ball."

15

ON SATURDAY I found Cat in her kitchen with markers and several sheets of paper. "We're going to make cootie catchers," she announced as she adjusted the volume on her transistor radio. "Don't worry, Ricky will be out with Dad on the boat all day."

"Cootie catchers?"

"They were popular in Portland and are great for making choices. Sometimes they're called fortune tellers." She showed me how to fold the paper corner to corner and then all points to the middle. We flipped it over and did it again until we both had a perfect cootie catcher to squeeze our fingers into, almost like a puppet's mouth.

"Now, on the outside you write four colors," said Cat. "On the next layer, put eight numbers, and on the inside, put answers to questions. Like, yes, no, maybe, no way, and so on."

We folded, creased, and created to the sounds of Casey Kasem's Top Forty. Between songs we could hear Mrs. Fantino typing her recipes in the other room. The day was so much fun that my problem began to seem like not such a big deal.

At one point, Cat jumped up. "I almost forgot, we've got Jiffy Pop!" She pulled out a silver pan-shaped package that had its own handle.

I joined her at the stove. "I've seen those on TV, but we've never tried them."

We each took turns shaking the aluminum pan back and forth in circles across the burner until the cover foil slowly unfolded and puffed up into a giant silver ball. I couldn't take my eyes off it, wondering if the foil would explode. The popcorn inside smelled delicious. Finally the popping slowed way down, and we removed it from the heat. Cat pricked the foil ball with a sharp knife and we both jumped back from the steam that escaped.

"Mhmm," said Cat. "I love this stuff." We grabbed handfuls of hot popcorn. Cat went back again and again. "I can't stop!" Then she made a sad face and looked down. "I really shouldn't eat so much. I'll be big as a house before I get out of high school, and then I'll *never* get a date."

"You look great. You're just big-boned," I said. "Let's take a walk later, and it will be like we never ate it."

We washed the oil off our fingers and then made another set of cootie catchers, this time with names inside. In anticipation of asking 'who should I go to the dance with?' I put Craig, Ricky, Cat, and..... "Cat! Who should I put on the last square? Oh, I know. I'll put myself on that one." Then I thought carefully. I came up with seven answers with an equal distribution of yeses and nos. One space left.

"Here, let me write it." Cat took my catcher and then covered it as she wrote. Her lips turned up in a sly grin.

"Hey, what are you writing in there?"

Cat smirked and then burst into giggles. "No peek-ing."

She slid the fortune teller across the table to me, but I had already picked up the first catcher I made, figuring I'd try it one more time.

I started right in with my question, squeezing the catcher back and forth with each letter of my chosen words. I opened the last flap and then looked up quick. "It came out 'most likely' for Craig."

"Do it again."

I did, asking my question slightly different and spelling lime green instead of yellow. "Ricky came out 'probably'." This is going to be a big help—not."

"Oh, wait," said Cat, "you're using the wrong catcher."

I picked up the second cootie catcher and snapped the pockets back and forth. First it came out Ricky, and then Craig.

"Again," said Cat giggling

I smiled. "This time it says I should go to the dance with Cat!"

"Again!" Cat screamed. She could barely control herself.

"This is really weird. How it comes out different every time."

Cat was silently figuring something in her head— "Spell orange for your last turn!"

I got to the last layer. "Huh? What?" I peered at what Cat had written. "Go with Archie? The cartoon character?"

Cat was hysterical by now. "Wouldn't that be a riot? And you have to admit he's cute."

"Yeh, right, and you can take his pal, Jughead." I sighed, stifled my grin, and pretended to scowl. "I'm trying to solve an important problem."

Cat finally caught her breath and ran out of laughter. "Hmpf," she said in a pompous voice. "I wouldn't know about such difficulties." Then, we both burst into giggles.

I sighed again. "Time for a break."

We took a long walk through the port and then returned to goof around with the cootie catchers some more. I loved the feel of the crisply folded paper wrapped around my fingers. However, I still hadn't figured out a solution to my problem. We asked other, more serious, questions, too, like whether Finn would be proven innocent. I could have cried when the answer showed as no. Before long we were back to discussing the upcoming art exhibit.

I left Cat's house late that afternoon, more confused than ever about what to do about the dance. How could I possibly have two dates? Me, Amy Henderson?

Soon I found myself at the pier, pacing the planks. The weather was mild for a change, and Finn had made good progress on his painting. Now he packed up his supplies for the day. I was glad he'd been able to get some time in on the pier *and* that we had the exhibit coming up soon—anything that kept his thoughts off the trial that would take place later in the month, was a good thing. We both had a little too much on our minds these days.

"You look like a nervous old tom cat," he said.

"Just trying to figure something out."

Finn scratched his whiskers. "I'm pretty good at puzzles."

What would Finn know about dances and dates? More to the point, my problem seemed trivial next to his. "That's okay, it's nothing." I continued to pace.

"Whoa," said Finn. "Watch where you're stepping there."

I scooted aside as he gently picked up a small pink starfish from the plank my sneaker had been ready to land on. He brought the starfish down to the shore of the beach and let it wiggle off his hand until it reached water. "There you go, little guy."

I helped Finn get his bundles into the boat and then watched him chug across to the island.

ON MONDAY, WHEN work at the library was particularly slow, I was glad to have a chance to talk with Mrs. Baldwin alone. I told her how Finn would have to appear in court.

"Yes, I heard about that. Such a talented man," she said. "It's a shame he let that fire get out of hand."

"He didn't do anything wrong."

"What? Who did it, then?" Mrs. Baldwin creased her brow, confused.

"I have no idea, but please believe me. Finn wouldn't hurt a fly. Mrs. Baldwin," I said, returning to the problem at hand. "We've got this exhibit coming up. I'm afraid no one will attend with all these rumors circling around."

Mrs. Baldwin pushed her glasses down to the end of her long nose and peered over the top of them at me. "I'm not completely convinced, nevertheless, if you say he's innocent, I'll hold my tongue. Accidents happen, I suppose." She went back to filing cards, and I thought the conversation had ended. Unfortunately, she still hadn't said whether she would come to the exhibit. I watched her for a minute and almost as though I had pushed the idea to speak, right into her head, she said, "I've got quite the busy weekend coming up. When did you say the exhibit was again?"

I regurgitated all the details for her. She had reserved the church hall for us, and there was a flyer hanging right across the room on the library bulletin board. Oh, well, it was worth repetition. If only she realized how important this event was and how it would keep Finn from having to feel lousy from now until the trial. It was out of my hands, though. I'd have to trust that a few people would find the time to show up on Saturday.

16

ON THURSDAY NIGHT, Mom came into the kitchen and found me rummaging through her recipe box. "What are you looking for, Honey?"

"I was hoping to make ginger cookies. The kind that Miss Cogshell used to make."

"I've never made those. Let's see, I'm sure there'll be a recipe in my *Betty Crocker's.*" Mom flipped through the big red binder. "Here's one for Ginger Creams."

I studied the recipe. "This might be close. Can I make them?" I reached up and got down the mixing bowl.

"Now, hold on, let's make sure we've got all the ingredients."

Turned out we had everything, but nutmeg, so we gave it a go. With Mom helping we got through in no time, *and* I avoided my usual baking disasters.

When the cookies were almost ready to come out of the oven, I inhaled a deep breath and then felt tears prick my eyes. "Perfect. It's like Miss Cogshell's kitchen used to smell."

Mom gave me a quick hug. "They do smell delicious." Ever since I'd lost Miss Cogshell, Mom seemed warmer, more frequent with the hugs. Or was it me who had changed? Maybe I'd come out of my shell, let her get closer now.

CAT, RICKY, AND I were so busy hanging and arranging paintings on Friday afternoon, I didn't get a chance to really appreciate our efforts—to step back and study the room with fresh eyes—until later. When I returned the next day, I was impressed. It looked like a professional show and other than the nice janitor who had set up chairs and swept the floor beforehand, we kids had made it happen.

Cat and I arrived at the same time, both with big plates of cookies in our arms. After we stirred up some soda and sherbet to make a pretty punch, we had time to kill. We pretended to be rich art connoisseurs.

"This little painting is simply *lovely,*" said Cat with an English accent. She pushed her glasses down to the tip of her nose and examined a small picture of seagulls poised against an ocean background.

"And look at this one." I raised my eyebrows and pursed my lips as my index finger pointed downward in a delicate motion. Finn's full signature: Finn Eriksson was neatly printed in the corner of each work.

We must have glanced at the door a hundred times. Finally, at about five past, there was a shuffling in the hallway. Yay! People! Buyers!

Nope.

"Over here, Ricky," I called out. "Squeeze in and find a seat amongst the crowd!"

Cat threw me a quick scowl. My mouth fell open as I realized she was afraid I had hurt someone's feelings. Ricky hadn't come in alone. Finn's hair was slicked back and his short beard was trimmed and tidy. He wore a blue suit, threadbare, but well-fitted, and even had on a necktie—red with sailboats.

I swallowed as my ears began to burn. "I'm sure it will fill up any minute now. Don't they look great?"

"Yep," said Cat. "Finn does look great, tie and all."

I smiled. "Of course, he does. Except I kind of meant the paintings."

Finn looked around at the walls covered with fine art, and nodded, a modest grin on his face.

Against one wall, like ducks at an arcade, the four of us sat in a row for going on half an hour. Cat and I exchanged worried expressions. When I'd reminded Mrs. Baldwin of the exhibit one more time, the day before, she told me she knew Finn couldn't be a pyro something or other and that she'd make sure he had a strong turnout. However sometimes, although she meant well, Mrs. Baldwin didn't always follow through.

Ricky tried to fill the empty silence. "I really like how you paint boats," he said. "Are they hard to do?"

"Nope," said Finn. "Boats are pretty easy. I just paint 'em as I see 'em." He stood up and pointed towards one of the larger landscapes. "Now, sky and water—those are trickier. Not so easy to get all them shades of blue lookin' natural." He squinted at the painting. "Sometimes I hit it close." He sighed and then sat back down beside us on the squeaky metal chairs.

Not long after, like the sound of thunder at the end of a drought, we heard footsteps coming down the hall. Lots of footsteps. Mrs. Baldwin paused at the entrance to the room, a large brimmed hat on her head, and then strode over to us, followed by a crowd of equally fancy women. I breathed a deep sigh of relief and gratitude.

"Mr. Eriksson," she said, "I'd like you to meet the Greater Port Wells Garden Club. The Arts and Crafts group is on their way." No sooner had she said it, then I heard an echo of the previous thunder—*click clack click clack*—high heels on wooden floors. And in trooped local artists and craftsmen to fill the room, as well. A few of the older members came right up to Finn. Apparently, they had been trying to get him to join their group for years, but he'd always been too busy out at the lighthouse.

I will never forget watching the most elegant citizens of Port Wells, along with fine-looking visitors from several surrounding towns, study the paintings of my friend. Some of the club ladies brought their husbands, too.

The men gathered about a lobster boat scene in particular, with great interest. I couldn't have been prouder if I'd painted them all myself. They ooh'd and ahh'd and murmured their approval. Because they all arrived at once, a little competition began.

"This would look nice in my parlor," said one heavy-set woman eyeing a large painting of boats in the harbor.

A blonde woman rushed over and nearly shoved her out of the way. "No, Blanche, it's a perfect match for *my* new drapes and sofa."

I caught Cat's eye, and we both had to rush to the tiny kitchen off of the exhibit hall to erupt into giggles.

"Did you see her?" I was laughing so hard, I could barely get the words out. "She pu. . .pushed the other woman!"

Cat gasped for air. "Oh, my gosh, I can't breathe."

Finally we got ourselves under control, smoothed down our skirts, and re-entered the room.

My parents and Mr. and Mrs. Fantino had arrived by then, bringing the number up to 37 visitors. Nancy had an 'away' game to cheer at, but she had wished me luck before she went.

"What a lovely exhibit," said my mother with a wink. "This must have been a lot of work for someone."

"Cat and I did it," I said. "And Ricky, too, he made all the frames."

"You kids did all this, Amy?" said my father. He and my mother exchanged proud glances and then Dad chuckled. "I thought I smelled cookies baking the other night. I came out into the kitchen after you'd gone to bed, but I couldn't find them, didn't realize they'd be here."

I laughed. I'd hidden the wrapped cookies up in my room after they'd cooled, just in case.

Dad continued to look around. "Everything looks great, paintings all spread out to fill the room, very impressive." Glancing at my mother, he said, "Amy's a chip off the old block."

Mom blushed. "I guess I *am* a pretty good hostess and party planner, too."

"Yep," agreed Dad.

EVEN CRAIG DROPPED by. I couldn't believe it. I brought him right over to meet Finn. They shook hands—one tall and towheaded and the other gristly and bewhiskered.

"Cool work you've got here," said Craig.

Finn looked up into Craig's grinning face and like most people do, I could tell he liked him right off.

Shortly after, when Craig went to stand in front of my favorite ocean scene, I was quick to join him.

"Wow, this is almost as good as looking at the real thing from the pier," said Craig.

"I love this one, too," I said.

"Only one thing missing."

I peered at the painting. "What's that?"

Craig pointed halfway out across the water. "There should be a little seal right about here."

"That would be cool. Pup and his friend could both be in the picture. I'll put a request in to Finn."

Craig grinned. "I bet you will."

"That's one of my favorites, too," said Ricky, suddenly beside me.

"You probably don't see it quite the same, though," said Craig. "Ya know, being a city boy and all."

Ricky always acted a little nervous when Craig was around. I watched him stick out his bottom lip a smidgen and push up his glasses before he said, "Just because I used to live in Portland, doesn't mean I'm not a downeaster, through and through. I was born, bred, and buttered in Maine."

I laughed at his clever play on words.

Craig grinned and patted Ricky on the shoulder. "I know you were. Don't get your boxers in a twist."

I rolled my eyes and moved over a few feet. "So, Craig, what do you think of Ricky's frames?" I'd do anything to get the conversation away from boys' underwear.

"You made these?" Craig looked from wall to wall. "All of them?"

Ricky raised his chin, not as self-conscious looking as before.

Craig nodded his approval. "Very cool. I was telling our girl here that I could get into the idea of working with wood."

I hid a grin, picturing myself being *their* girl. Craig sometimes had a way of making people feel special.

"I like the smell of wood shavings," Craig continued. "Maybe I'll try a frame." He gave Ricky a light punch in the arm. "Wouldn't that be something? We'd be like two peas in a pod."

I laughed and moved to the next wall of paintings. Ricky and Craig stayed where they were, continuing their conversation about woodworking. Great, maybe they'd become friends after all.

From where I stood, I could hear whispers across the room, and I had a sense of being watched. I backed up a few inches as though to admire the painting and at the same time turned my position to the left. Two women stood by the punch bowl. I hadn't noticed them before or even seen them come in. They were actually staring past me, at Finn, as their mouths flapped a hundred miles an hour. I didn't like the look of the scowl on the tall, skinny one. Without a moment's hesitation, I sped to the refreshments table like a dehydrated camel.

I came up behind them and listened to their conversation as I slowly dipped the ladle into the bowl and scooped up a serving of brightly-colored, fizzy punch.

"Mildred insisted I come along. Unfortunately, I didn't realize until I got here that the painter and the arsonist were one and the same," said the beak-nosed taller woman.

Her partner in hearsay nodded vigorously as her jowls shook in time. "To think what might have happened. He could have burned down the whole port."

"Well, I for one won't be spending a dime on the likes of him," said the first woman.

As they both sniffed in agreement, I could feel myself getting hotter than a boiled lobster in a pot. Anger steamed up from my toes. I knew I was going to do something, and it wasn't going to be pretty. There was no stopping me now. I took a step towards them.

17

"EXCUSE ME," I said boldly to the women gossiping about Finn. They both turned around to face me. Okay, good start, but now what? My knees began to shake. "I um, I couldn't help but overhear you."

"Yes?" The skinny lady raised her eyebrows.

"Finn is not an arsonist. He didn't set the woodshed fire."

"Oh? Who did?"

Now my face was on fire itself. What had I gotten myself into? I could barely find my words; however, I pushed them out as best I could. "Um, I'm not sure. But please know he's innocent. Come to the trial. When Finn is let off. . .um. . ..”

The two women stared at me, silent and disapproving, until I figured out how to finish my sentence.

"Yes, that's right." I made my voice stronger. "When Finn is proven innocent, all of these paintings will skyrocket in value."

That got their attention. "Really?" The busybodies looked like they didn't believe me, although they did take a peek around at the walls. The shorter woman's jowls began to shake as she prepared to speak. Then both pairs of eyes suddenly shot up to look beyond where I stood, their mouths clamping shut faster than lobster claws.

From behind me came Craig's deep confident voice. "Yep, I'd snap them up quick. I just got back from Boston, and I'd say these are going to be a *hot-t-t* commodity."

The ladies exchanged a last glance and then practically fell over each other trying to get to an unsold painting first.

I let out a breath of air. "Whew."

Craig stood there staring at me.

"What?" I said when I got my voice back.

"Nothing." He shook his head and grinned. "You're just really something else."

"Is that good?"

"Yep. It's good all right. When I think of you a year ago. Or at least what I thought you were like—always so quiet and kind of aloof."

I could feel my stubborn pride perk up at the possible insult. I mean I was always me inside, except I hadn't let anyone in to see me.

"Not anymore. You're a real go-getter now."

I smiled at Craig. "Commodity? Isn't that kind of a big word for you?"

"Nope. I'm full of surprises."

"*Touché.*"

There wasn't much clean up to do, and we encouraged Finn through the door before it became too dark out on the water. He left with a jingle in his pocket and an ear-to-ear grin. The paintings would remain on exhibit for another few weeks and then the lucky new owners could display them in their homes.

Cat and Ricky had to leave promptly, too. They were surprising their dad with a little birthday cake that night and still needed to get things ready.

Therefore, while my parents talked with the last of the guests, it was only me and Craig left.

Although he had definitely changed over his time away, when Craig wasn't with the school crowd, I still felt I could talk with him about anything. I told him how worried I was about the upcoming court trial. "I keep telling everyone Finn is innocent, but what if he's…" I found I couldn't even say the word guilty in reference to my friend. "What if he's not?" I stammered. "What if they throw him in jail?

"I have no doubt, Amy, with you on his side, he'll do fine."

"Will you be there?" I asked.

"Nope, sorry. I'm still catching up in school. I've gotta be home with my little brother and sisters right after, anyway. My old lady's meeting with her counselor that day."

"Oh, of course, I understand."

"She's doing good. I think she's going to beat this thing." Craig tapped his fingers lightly against my head. "Knock on wood."

I jerked away and laughed. "That's wonderful."

"I've told her about you, ya know. How you and Miss C. got me through last year."

"I didn't do much."

Craig nodded. "You did a lot. You were my friend. If I was as levelheaded as you, I could probably do anything. You're kind of unique I guess."

"Unique?"

Craig laughed. "Yep, you're a rare commodity." He hesitated and shoved his hair up out of his eyes. "Am I still using that *big* word right, Teach? Anyways, it's good you don't follow the crowd." Then his face looked more serious as he moved closer to the door. "Don't ever change," he threw back over his shoulder. Craig took off and left me to my parents who also appeared ready to leave.

I considered his last weird words. They didn't make sense. Why would I ever change? Was my face that easy to read? Could he tell my brain usually went to mush whenever he was around? At least he hadn't brought up the dance, since I still didn't know how to answer. Or, yikes, maybe he forgot he asked me. No time to dwell on it now, it was time to think about the trial.

AS MY PARENTS and I walked home from the exhibit together, I said, "Dad, would you be able to drive Cat and me to Finn's trial?"

"That's on a Tuesday, right?"

"Yes, a week from this coming Tuesday." I crossed my fingers as we walked. Pale golden light and wisps of scented wood smoke reached out to us from the few homes we passed.

My mother shot me a look. "Don't you have school that day?"

"Well, sort of, except this seems more important."

"It is important," Mom said with a sigh. "With all the talk that goes on around here, I'm afraid of the outcome. In fact, I'm not too sure you should be quite so involved, Amy."

I started to panic, then I looked at Dad, who was studying me.

"Actually," he said, with a glance at Mom. "I wouldn't mind attending as well. I'm sure it will turn out fine, but in case they suddenly need to pull in character witnesses, I'd like to be there, for what it's worth. Being a loner, Finn probably doesn't have too many people rooting for him."

Whew. I let out the breath I'd been holding. Then I puckered my brow. "Is that a yes?"

My father grinned. "Yes. It's my roundabout way of replying in the affirmative."

I rolled my eyes and then jumped up to slap a tree as we passed by. "Yay!"

"Amy, I hope you realize that no matter how much you want Mr. Eriksson to be innocent, it may not turn out the way you wish."

I stopped leaping in mid-air and felt a scowl forming. "He has to be innocent."

"Dad's right," said Mom. "Only one person was in the woodshed, using a stove."

How dare they say my deepest fears out loud? Did my parents really both feel Finn might have started the fire? He would never hurt anything. I remembered the little lumpy starfish Finn had tenderly slid into the sea. I bit my lip to keep from crying and made sure I walked in front of my parents for the rest of the way home.

"How is Finn getting to the courthouse?" Dad asked when we reached our door.

I halted in my tracks. I had figured he'd take the mail boat across and then maybe the bus, although now that I thought about it, he'd need to leave earlier than that to be on time. "I have no idea."

"We'll have an extra seat in the car. Please extend an invitation."

18

FIRST THING SUNDAY morning, I hit the pier. With the newly acquired praise of his talent, Finn was already painting up a storm despite the frosty air. Literally. Gray storm clouds swept across his canvas.

"Finn," I called out. "Do you need a ride to the courthouse next week?"

"Oh, I'm all set." He put down the paintbrush and rubbed his hands together for warmth. "A taxi will meet me down here after I zip across the bay in my boat."

I shook my head. "Not a good plan. What if it rains or snows? You'll look a mess before you even get there."

I looked across to the island. "How about you stay over at our house the night before, and then you can ride with us?"

"I couldn't impose." Then he looked up quick. "You're going? To the trial?"

"Yes, of course. I wouldn't miss it. Cat and I will be there, and my father's coming, too. He wants you to go with us."

Finn thought it over some more and finally decided it would be better than his plan. "Amy, girl, you're always thinking."

I left Finn to his work and checked the water as far as I could see in all directions. The end of the wharf was empty except for gulls perched on one side. I took a deep breath of fresh salt air. Between Craig's return and then both his and Ricky's invitation to the dance, it had been a busy couple of weeks.

Finn began to pack up.

"Are you all done for the day?" I said.

"Good stopping point. Too cold for this ol' geezer."

Finn got into his boat. I zipped my jacket up to my chin and watched him head for the island, zooming in and out of whitecaps and colorful buoys until he faded into the distant landscape.

The sound of a truck made me turn to see the harbormaster rumbling past on his rounds. As I started to turn back towards the water, something caught my eye. Although the library was closed, someone had just disappeared around the corner of the building. My body tensed, as it filled with a sense of protection for the library. There was no reason for anyone to be in the yard when it was closed, and I knew Mrs. Baldwin was visiting her grandchildren for the day. That, I could hardly forget. She had showed me all of their pictures for the tenth time this month and had gone on and on about her plans. Those kids were lucky they had such an energetic grandma to dote on them.

Then I felt the back of my neck tingle. While I stood gaping, the library might be getting vandalized. There was only one thing to do—check it out.

I crossed over from the pier and walked along the cobbled path. I peeked through an opening between a bush and the corner of the library, to the backyard. Nobody. Oh, well. Maybe my eyes were playing tricks on me. I adjusted the lobster buoys that hung beside the door. Sometimes they looked a little crooked. Then I heard whispering.

Or at least it sounded like whispering from this distance. My senses heightened. A sharp cidery scent came from the old apple tree in the far corner of the yard. I moved along the back of the library and then slowly peered around to the other side of the house.

Pamela and Claire sat on the grass with their backs against the clapboard wall. They puffed on cigarettes like old pros. Before I could pull my head back behind the building, they spotted me.

"Shrimp?" said Claire. "Are you spying on us?"

Ugh. That old nickname again. I'd probably be stuck with it forever.

Pamela joined in. "Yoo hoo, peek a boo."

In hindsight, I should have walked away, except my feet felt stuck to the ground. As a result I stayed planted and gawked.

Pamela attempted a smoke ring—lopsided, yet still impressive enough for Claire to toss the end of her cigarette down and applaud wildly.

"That could start a fire." I pointed at the tossed butt.

Pamela laughed. "What did you say?"

And then it hit me. "You were smoking behind the woodshed, weren't you? The night it burned down."

Pamela and Claire both leaped up and charged over to where I was standing. Although I'd grown two inches this year, they still towered above me. "No, Shrimp." Pamela wagged her finger at me. "We did *not* burn down the woodshed. And don't you forget it. It was that crazy old painter who did it."

I inched backward. They were there that night. Finn had heard them talking outside right before the fire. It all made sense now.

Claire squashed the discarded cigarette with the toe of her boot.

Pamela moved closer to me. So close, I could smell her Dippity-do hair gel. "You tell anyone—," she scowled and made a fist at me, "and you'll be dead meat. One punch, and I could smash your nose right off your face."

I felt my lip quiver and bit down hard on it. The last thing I wanted to do was to let Pamela think she could bully me, but inside I knew I was petrified. I still remembered how in fifth grade she had beat up one of the boys—hurt him bad enough that he had to miss school for a week.

Pamela took the last step between us until I felt shoved up against the wall. Knowing there was no escape, I could barely breathe. I wished Howard the harbormaster could somehow magically appear and save me.

After what felt like forever, Pamela stepped back and brushed her hands together as though we had settled something. She continued to stare at me with an amused smirk on her glossy pink lips. "Where's your chunky little friend?"

Claire laughed. "Meow, meow."

"So, like, why did they move here anyway?" Pamela continued. "Trouble? Did they need a *fresh* start?"

My fear turned to anger. Cat was one of the kindest, most generous people I'd ever met. How dare they talk about her that way? They didn't deserve any information concerning Cat *or* her family. I would never add to their gossip or anyone else's. Didn't they realize it took as much energy, courage, and cleverness to be kind as it did to be cruel and that every little action made a difference? In the past I'd watched how their faces lit up whenever they discussed someone's misfortune, even if it was the poor luck of one of their own so-called friends. They never seemed to care if someone had good news to share. No way would I tell them anything. Ever, I decided. Good *or* bad.

I sidestepped fast and got myself around the rest of the corner. Then I bolted across the yard to the sounds of their laughter. I assumed I was going home, but next thing I knew I stood gasping for breath on Cat's back step. I guess I hadn't thought to go to Craig because he'd only met Finn the one time at the exhibit. Besides, I was much more comfortable at the Fantinos' house. The memory of Craig's drunken mother, pretty as she was, still gave me the creeps.

Ricky answered my knock. His face brightened when he saw me. "Amy! Come on in."

"Where's Cat?" As I spoke, Cat entered the kitchen to join us.

I huffed and puffed a minute. "I think I've got evidence."

"Huh?" said Ricky. They both looked at me with confusion.

"The woodshed fire. I know who started it." Then I slumped into a kitchen chair. "But, no proof."

"Really?" Cat's eyes got wide.

Usually, I found it easy to confide in Cat and Ricky, except now something stopped me. As I was about to blurt out Pamela's and Claire's names, I realized the error of my ways. Not only did Pamela have a ton of relatives, but because her mother was the postmistress, the Johnsons knew everyone in town. Even Mrs. Baldwin was good friends with Sally Johnson.

"You can't breathe a word of this," I said. "To anyone!"

"But who did it?" said Cat. "Can't you tell us?"

"Shouldn't the police know?" said Ricky. "I mean, in case they *did* start the fire?"

I shook my head adamantly. "No, they'll kill me! And like I said, I haven't any proof. You've got to swear you won't mention that I have a hunch." I continued to plead. They both looked doubtful, and I didn't feel very good about myself. Why, oh, *why* did I almost go and blab everything right after being threatened? Knowing Pamela, she'd drag everyone into this if she ever found out I'd told. And I couldn't bear to think of her teasing Cat.

In a small voice I said, "I'm not really certain after all. But somehow I'll find a way to make sure the truth comes out."

I waited in the silence of their cozy kitchen, amid leftover smells of toast and coffee, until Ricky finally nodded and said, "Okay, then. I promise."

"Me, too," said Cat. "But, let us know if you need help."

After making sure the coast was clear of bullies, I trudged home feeling the weight of the world on my shoulders. That night I had the worst nightmare I'd ever had. All these people were shouting at me. They told me to give up my information. I can't remember what I said in the dream, but next thing I knew, Pamela and Claire, both looking about ten feet tall, chased me. They each grabbed one of my arms and dragged me down a zillion steps into a dark chamber. Before I could figure out where I was or what type of monster made such a horrible, grinding roar, I bolted awake, screaming and sweaty. And relieved. Relieved that I had kept what I knew to myself.

19

FOR THE REST of the week, dingy clouds lay over the Port. By Saturday, I was ready to jump out of my skin. Only three more days until Finn's court appearance. There had been a public notice in the newspaper stating that two teenagers, most likely Pamela and Claire, were going to be asked questions; therefore, I felt certain the truth would be revealed. Still, something niggled at the back of my mind. I wished I'd known sooner about their smoking, soon enough to do something. I'd considered asking my father what he thought would happen if new evidence came out during the trial. I would have told him without mentioning names, of course. But he'd been wicked busy lately. Moreover, he was already being a nice guy to go at all, since he hardly knew Finn. If I said too much, he might decide Finn would be easily cleared and that we didn't need to be there at the courthouse for him, after all.

Unlike my own stifled jitters, Nancy had bounced around in her cheerleader uniform all morning. She'd finally left at the sound of a car horn outside because she had to be at the football stadium early; ahead of my parents who were also attending.

"Amy, why don't you come with us?" said my mother. "Dad and I are both going, and you've never seen your sister cheer."

Huh? All day Nancy had been yelling and clapping. "When *isn't* she cheering?" I muttered. "I've seen her cheer a zillion times."

"It's not the same. You'd enjoy watching her with the whole group of girls. They're quite good. Perhaps, it will inspire you to get involved in a couple of years."

"Mom. Are you serious? Do you really think I'm going to be a cheerleader?" I call it a lucky day if my teachers can hear me answer their questions, never mind an entire football stadium.

"Well," Mom said. "You never know."

"Yes, I do know. It's not going to happen. The last thing I'd want to do is dance around screaming in public in a little skirt."

Mom laughed and shook her head in exasperation. "Still, you're not doing anything, the sun's peeking out for a change, and it would mean a lot to your sister. There are only a handful of home games."

It was true. I didn't have a thing to do. Ever since Cat started running story time at the library, we both worked on alternating Saturdays, giving me more time off. My mind was way too full to even try to read a book. And I'd already drawn a face on the pumpkin Mom brought home from a farm stand the day before. Now it sat on our front step with its giant grin and triangle eyes, waiting for Halloween.

I sighed. Maybe getting out for a while would make the time pass faster and take my mind off my problems. "Okay, I'll go."

Soon we were on our way to the game. Dad and Mom in the front seat with me scrunched down in the back. A song came on the radio. One I'd never heard before, with a real catchy beat. The guy kept singing "keep on truckin'" over and over. My father turned down the volume, and my mother nodded in agreement. They didn't like any of the new stuff. I strained to hear every note and immediately decided it was my new favorite.

We rode past large patches of wilted brown land. I remembered back to my last weeks of the previous school year, when I would gaze out at these same fields through the bus windows. Except, then there were masses of purple lupines as far as I could see. If I closed my eyes, I could still picture them.

A few more miles and then the cutest cabins appeared after a curve in the road. A vacancy sign hung over the door of the main office. I'd always thought it would be fun to stay at this place because each of the eight cabins was painted a different bright color. Not the shades you'd find in nature, more like dazzling acrylic paint hues—orange, lemon, even purple. A matching striped buoy hung by the cabin doors. When customers checked in I wondered if they could make a request, such as: "We'd like the turquoise cabin, please."

It was a long ride, past more fields of cornstalks, and then through the city. I hummed the new trucking song to myself, but was still pretty carsick by the time we arrived. When I climbed out of the car, the crisp fall air brushed my queasiness away. I hadn't taken time to think about what going to the game with my parents might be like. As soon as we entered the stadium, I knew.

I could see gangs of kids from school in every direction. A big group from my grade passed close by us. And there was me. Good ol' Shrimp with her mommy and daddy on either side of her. We might as well have been holding hands. I tried to shrink down smaller and disappear.

Finally, we found seats on the bleachers.

"Is this a good spot, Amy?" said Dad in a loud voice.

"Shh." I sat down hard on the cold bench and slumped.

As we watched the game, I tried to figure out what was going on. All padded up, the players looked bloated and kind of stupid—like overgrown toddlers crashing into each other as they tried to get hold of the little ball. Strong smells of popcorn and hotdogs filled the air. Then finally it was halftime, and the cheerleaders came running out again to do a special routine. I had to admit Nancy did well. She blended right in with the others. All the girls had huge smiles and full, swinging ponytails. At one point Nancy looked right up at me and grinned. I gave her a quick thumbs-up back.

Although a scraggly bunch, I also enjoyed watching the marching band attempt to play a few popular songs. They didn't sound half bad when they performed "These Eyes." Not nearly as good as *The Guess Who* band, but still pretty decent.

In the middle of the second half of the game I realized that Pamela and Claire were seated in the first row of bleachers, right behind the cheerleaders. Were they nervous about the trial, too? I decided if they looked my way, and if I dared, I'd give them a real stink eye, to show I was on to them. Instead, I watched them do some of the hand motions and cheers from their seats—a regular little pep squad. By then I was frozen and sitting on my own hands to keep warm.

Finally, the game was over. I knew this because everybody started shouting and jumping up. We'd won. As we were climbing down from the bleachers, I noticed Pamela and Claire went over to the left and joined a large huddle of kids. I could have sworn I saw the top of Craig's head in the middle of the group. A thin wisp of smoke circled above them.

Oh well. Home we went. I'd done my duty, and, of course, I'd be sure to tell Nancy she had done a good job.

20

MONDAY FOUND ME back in school, and in my usual seat during math class—a few rows behind and to the left of Pamela. Seemed to be my new hobby, staring at the back of her head. I'd had butterflies in my stomach all day; however, she didn't look nervous in the least. When I'd found that small notice about the case in the previous week's newspaper, at first I was relieved to read that two teenage girls would also be questioned. Except now I wondered, *wait a minute, who told?* Even if Ricky and Cat suspected I had evidence against Pamela and Claire, they had both promised not to say a word. No, it couldn't have been them. It *must* have been somebody else. Right? Who else could know? Would Pamela and Claire think I tattled on them?

I regretted not telling my parents everything I knew. Except what did I really know? Just because I'd caught Pamela and Claire smoking didn't mean they were the ones who lit the fire, any more than it meant Finn had.

Then a worse idea struck me. What if it wasn't Pamela and Claire the article referred to, at all? Could one of the girls be me? I shook that thought from my head faster than a deer fly ready to bite.

AFTER MATH CLASS I went to my locker and found Pamela already there, waiting for me. She squinted her eyes. "Why were you gawking at me all through class?"

Gosh, she had to have eyes on the back of her head to know I was looking at her during math. Then I remembered Claire sat in the row behind me. Great, she must have snitched.

Hands on hips as she let out an exasperated sigh, Pamela waited for my explanation.

"I wasn't." I fiddled with the combination of my locker and hoped like anything she'd go away.

Pamela took a step towards me. "Yuh, you were."

This conversation was doing nothing to help my nervous stomach. In fact, I worried I'd puke, right there on the spot.

"I, uh. . .I guess I was wondering if you were going to be in court tomorrow," I stammered.

Pamela tossed her hair back and greeted some guy going past us. When he was out of hearing distance, she hissed, "Why should I go to court?"

A new wave of nausea swept over me. If Pamela really wasn't going, how could Finn be let off? "Because you were there," I said quietly, "the night of the fire."

Pamela rolled her eyes and shifted from one foot to the other. "Actually, I *am* going, if it's any of your business."

Relief washed away my queasy feelings, and I proceeded to work my combination lock.

Pamela moved in closer. "Everyone knows Claire and me had nothing to do with the fire. Everyone. It was that old freak who set it. And if any little snitch says differently, they'll be in huge trouble." Leaving a whiff of perfume, she stormed away.

I WAS STILL a mess by the time I got to the library that afternoon. After I made a couple of silly mistakes, Mrs. Baldwin said, "Is everything okay, Amy?"

I nodded. "Although I *am* worried about the court case tomorrow. I'm hoping the right people get charged with the crime."

"The right people?"

"Well, you know, whoever lit the fire."

"Finn?"

"No, not him."

Mrs. Baldwin creased her brow, confused. "You realize, Amy, if you have information about this, you are required to speak up. As your civic obligation, of course."

A vision of Pamela shoving me through a meat grinder filled my mind. I looked down at the book I was shelving: *The Exorcist*. How appropriate. I hadn't even dared glance at the summary on the back cover, never mind read the book. I jammed the paperback into place on the shelf.

"Telling the truth could possibly be the only thing that keeps your friend on the right side of the law," Mrs. Baldwin continued.

I swallowed and nodded. How did I always manage to get in over my head with problems? "Yes, of course. I won't let anything happen to Finn."

Besides, maybe nobody had told my secret. Maybe Pamela and Claire were coincidentally two of many people being questioned. Once they took the stand inside the courtroom, the judge would swear them in and then they would have to tell the truth. All would be resolved.

LATER THAT AFTERNOON, as predicted, the day turned cold and rainy—a raw, dark warning of winter. Finn arrived at our house, looking more nervous than a fish on a line and had about as much to say. On my way upstairs I overheard my parents talking in their room— whispering something about it being too late now to do anything about it. About what? I wondered. Had they found out something I didn't know? I spent half the night on my window seat. I peered out into the dark woods and prayed that Finn would be cleared of all crimes.

I WOKE TO the smell of bacon and coffee. Tuesday had arrived. We all ate what we could and then went to pick up Cat. She rushed out to the car between raindrops, her long braid swinging. I was grateful we both got to miss school for the day in order to support Finn. It was a quiet ride into town—Dad and Finn in the front seat and us kids in the rear. A light rain kept the windshield wipers busy. *Click swoosh, click swoosh,* back and forth.

Halfway through the trip, Dad cleared his throat. Then he carefully said to Finn, "Do you feel you have good representation?"

Finn pulled at his chin whiskers. "You mean a lawyer?"

"Yes. Does the lawyer the court appointed for you seem pretty good?"

"Oh, that. Well, sounds like there *will* be someone nearby. They mentioned about it at the arraignment, but somehow my paperwork never made it onto the mail boat." Finn nodded in a nervous way. "Yep, I'll be pretty much representing myself."

I watched my father's face. He was chewing on the inside of his lip which usually meant he had something to say, but was holding back.

Dad dropped us off and then went to park the car. "Good luck in there, Finn," he said.

The rain had paused and the three of us—Cat, Finn, and I, slowly climbed the wide cement steps leading up to the front entrance of the brick courthouse. By the time we reached the second floor courtroom, my father had caught up. He still had a worried look, a furrowed brow.

We found seats, and then I watched Finn find his place at the front, beyond the railing that separated us.

I was sitting with Cat on one side and my father on the other in the first row of spectators.

"Is it going to be okay, Dad?" I whispered.

"Let's hope so," was all he said.

Because I knew that others had been called in to testify, I was sure Finn would be off the hook. But what was all this about lawyers and no lawyers? The teenagers had to be Pamela and Claire. Although I still didn't know if someone had turned them in or if everyone at the scene was being questioned. If the former, I sure hoped they wouldn't think I had anything to do with the fire.

I looked around the courtroom for Pamela and Claire, and my eyes landed on two girls who looked about as much like them as I did. Their makeup-free faces were scrubbed clean, no hoop earrings, no teased hair. And they both had crisp shirts with button-down collars fastened right up to their chins. They actually looked sweet. The churning in my stomach grew stronger.

"Oh." Cat nudged my elbow. "I meant to tell you that Ricky said he'd be sending good luck vibes. He wanted you to know that he would have been here if it wasn't for his French exam."

I nodded. "Tell him thanks. Finn needs all the help he can get."

Compared to what I'd seen on TV, it was a small courtroom. As it should be of course; it wasn't as if he'd been accused of murder. Three squeaky overhead fans pushed the stale air back and forth.

The solemnity brought tears to my eyes. As I waited, I became more and more worried about Finn. He sat up there in front, the center of attention, in the same suit and tie he had worn to the exhibit.

I heard a slight shuffling and turned my head to see all the ladies of the Greater Port Wells Arts and Crafts group coming through the door. Mrs. Baldwin organized them onto a long bench of seats. In spite of my nervousness, I grinned inside. No way were they going to let their newly purchased paintings go down in value. An artist painted them, not a criminal.

Everything went quiet when the black-robed judge entered the room.

"Do you swear to tell the truth, the whole truth, and nothing but the truth, so help you God?" The judge's deep voice echoed off the wood walls.

They got right to the opening statements for both sides and then moved on to the defendant.

"Now, Mr. Eriksson, may I call you Finn?" said the judge.

"Certainly. That's my name," said Finn.

Be careful, Finn. I crossed my fingers for good luck. All I wanted was for everyone to love Finn as much as I did. Unfortunately, there was always the possibility his salty ways might get misunderstood.

"Now, you were the lighthouse keeper on Wàwàckèchi Island up until last year. Is that correct?"

Finn nodded.

"Please answer with yes or no."

The judge waited.

"Yes," said Finn.

"And where are you living now?"

"On Wàwàckèchi."

153

"Do you have a house there?"

"I live in the keeper's hut at the lighthouse."

"Even though you are no longer the keeper?"

The judge waited. "Answer the question, please."

"I've already answered that one. You said it yourself. I was the keeper until last year."

"Then how can you still live there?"

"I do odds and ends. We have a deal," said Finn.

"Who has a deal?"

Finn sighed. "The Coast Guard and myself."

"Are you sure you're not trespassing?"

Finn straightened, defiant. "I've been tending that lighthouse for thirty years." He turned to a nearby man with a shaved head.

"Objection," said the man. With that, I figured out he must be Finn's lawyer. It was about time he spoke up, in my opinion. I was getting a headache—flashing my eyes back and forth between Finn and the judge— while I waited for each question and response. "This case is about a structure on Port Wells, not on Wàwàckèchi Island," said the bald man.

"Objection denied."

Question after question was fired at Finn. The confidence that shone so bright at his exhibit was waning now.

"What were you doing in that woodshed? Did you belong there? Were you using matches?"

"Yes. I used a match to light the woodstove." Finn looked around the courtroom with a helpless expression. "I was just heating up a can of beans for my damn supper."

Everyone around us drew in their breath. The lawyer guy shook his head in dismay. Watch out, Finn, I prayed.

21

FINALLY THE INTERROGATION ended, and the case moved on to other witnesses.

Fire Chief Sorensen showed some photos to the judge. He explained that the fire appeared to have started at ground level because of the v-shaped charred area discovered on what was left of the woodshed.

While the judge looked at the pictures, I looked at Cat. "That's good, right?" I whispered. "If the fire started at the base, then it couldn't be the stove."

"Unless the match intended for the stove landed on the floor." Cat frowned and chewed her lip. "I wonder which side of the ground the chief meant, inside or outside?"

I shrugged and turned to my father. "Why isn't the man beside Finn helping him? Isn't he the lawyer?"

"Yes, however, it looks like Finn wants to do this on his own, aside from that one objection." My father glanced to the front of the courtroom and then continued in a hushed voice. "There may be a charge if it doesn't go well. If he's found guilty, Finn probably can't afford to compensate for any service the standby counsel gives. Unless Finn asks for help, I think the lawyer has to remain silent—especially with the paperwork mix-up that Finn mentioned." He shook his head. "I wish I'd been on top of this."

"SALLY JOHNSON, PLEASE come to the stand."

Mrs. Johnson looked back at her husband nervously and then took her place and swore to the oath.

"Now, Mrs. Johnson, you were the one who called in the fire. Is that correct?" said the judge.

"Yes, that's right. I'd forgotten my purse at the post office after closing up for the day and when I returned that evening to get it, I noticed an odd smell. 'Why that smells like something burning,' I said. Working on my own all day gets me to talking to myself at times. Although, of course, people often come in to collect their mail."

"Stick to the necessary details only, please."

"Oh, yes. Of course." She wiggled one finger into her ear, as she was known to do. "Well, I looked down the lane and saw a thin wisp of smoke from in back of Sylvia Cogshell's old place. Her home is now our town library. I ran back inside the post office and dialed Stan, up at the firehouse."

"Did you see anyone or anything unusual?"

"Ayup. I went back outside and rushed right down to see if I could be of any assistance. Old Finn there," she pointed at Finn. "Well, he was lugging all this stuff out through the woodshed door. Got it out right before the fire burst into more flames. He skedaddled over to the trees with his bundle, set it down, and got to coughing. Next thing I knew the fire engine arrived. I looked at my watch and said, 'That's mighty fast timing'."

As I already knew, Sally Johnson didn't miss much that went on in the Port.

"Did you see your daughter Pamela anywhere near the property while all this was going on?"

I sat up straighter and waited for her answer.

Mrs. Johnson looked like a mother bird with a worm hidden in her mouth, as she darted a look towards Pamela and then back to the judge. She cleared her throat.

"Are you having trouble with the question, Mrs. Johnson?" said the judge.

"Oh, no, not at all. I did see Pammy. About the time the fire engine arrived, she and her little friend, Claire, such a nice girl; they were coming up from the pier. I imagine to see what all the commotion was about. And to see if they could help, of course."

Pamela smiled angelically at her mother and then at the judge. Oh, brother. This wasn't looking good at all.

When it was Pamela's turn to stand up, I had a full view of her. And with me being in the first row, she had a full view of me, too. I started to scrunch down in my seat, but then sat up tall again, so she'd know I meant for justice to be served.

"Please tell the court what happened on the evening in question."

I watched Pamela shift uncomfortably. "We watched them put out the fire."

"What were you doing before that?"

"Sitting on the grass. Talking."

"Where were you sitting?"

After some hesitation, she said quietly, "Outside the woodshed. We were so surprised to see someone come out of there." She sniffed. "We jumped up and ran."

"Somewhat recently, an empty package of Camels was found behind the library. Do you happen to smoke?"

Pamela looked around at the faces surrounding her, never landing on mine.

"No, um, I do not smoke. . . Camels."

I thought back to the day I'd caught Pamela and Claire smoking behind the library. I closed my eyes and could see the pack of cigarettes lying on the grass next to them. It was Lucky Strikes.

"Were you smoking on the night of the fire?" asked the judge.

Pamela squirmed in her seat, but remained silent.

The judge, obviously running out of patience, gave a great sigh. "Answer the question, Miss Johnson."

"The Camels package wasn't mine."

"Regardless of brands, do you smoke?" boomed the judge. There was an audible gasp in the courtroom.

Pamela paused and slowly started to shake her head no.

Oh, my gosh, she was going to lie on the witness stand! Seeing that one moment of faltering, I knew with every ounce of my being that they really had been smoking beside the woodshed that night. With all her connections, Pamela would probably only get a slap on the wrist, but who knows what they'd do to Finn. Kick him out of the Lighthouse Keeper's place? Make him owe so much that he couldn't paint anymore? Throw him in jail? Would she really let Finn be blamed for her mistake? Would *I?* I thought of how Craig had told me I was a real go-getter.

Before I even realized what I was doing, I shot up from my seat. My father's umbrella, which had been on the bench beside me, went crashing to the floor. In the silent courtroom it sounded like a gunshot and made

Pamela, and everyone else in the room, turn towards me. I looked directly at her and she stared back at me like a trapped rat. I wanted to speak, except the words stuck in my throat in the same way the truth appeared to be stuck in Pamela.

Our eyes were locked for what seemed hours, although it was probably only a few seconds. Then the judge said, "Please remain seated, or you will be asked to leave." I felt Cat tug on my pant leg as he gave me a stern look. I fell back onto the hard bench.

I continued to stare at Pamela. A lone tear slid down her cheek, and for the slightest moment I found myself forgetting who she was and all the pain she had caused me over the years. I almost felt sorry for her. By the time she spoke her face was red and splotchy. Then she mumbled something inaudible, and I snapped out of it.

Cat, oblivious to the turmoil in my brain, whispered in my ear. "She should be saying 'yes, your Honor'."

The judge continued to wait for Pamela. "Speak up, please," he said. He tapped his fingers twice on the desktop, his patience wearing thin.

"Yes," Pamela said again, louder. "Yes, we were smoking."

Mrs. Johnson's hands flew to her mouth. I heard a collective intake of breath from where the rest of Pamela's relatives sat behind us. I let out my own breath and could feel my dad's eyes on me. I ventured a peek.

He grinned and looked proud even though he couldn't have known the secret I had carried these past days.

I felt myself relax. My wishes had been answered. She was finally telling the truth. If she hadn't, it would have been up to me to tell the court what I knew, despite Pamela's threats for me to keep silent. I forced my eyes back on Pamela.

She stuck her lip out, and I recognized some of her old spunk. "Yes, we were smoking, and I *think* I might have thrown my cigarette in the grass." She looked surprised at her own words and swung her mane of hair around to stare at Claire, who sat in the seats behind her. Claire kept her eyes fixed on her lap and offered no help.

Pamela tried again. "I meant to say maybe. I mean, I'm not sure." Pamela rolled her eyes, and then her lip quivered. "I was so startled and afraid that we'd get cau. . .."

Whispered comments could be heard from all corners of the courtroom. The judge rapped his gavel for order to be retained, and then they continued with cross examinations. Claire took the stand briefly to confirm all that Pamela had admitted to.

The judge announced there would be a short recess while he considered the evidence.

We stayed in our seats. I looked down at my lap and saw that Cat had her fingers crossed beside me. I sighed and did the same. Other than the squeaking fans, the courtroom was silent. I looked over to where Finn sat. His head was slightly bowed, as though refusing to see anyone—ready to accept whatever was decided.

Next I studied Pamela and Claire. Were they worried? A group of Pamela's relatives had moved up to crowd around her. They were city people who looked like they could buy out our whole port. I noticed the flashy jewelry on a woman who was the spitting image of our postmistress—well—if Sally had a makeover. The fancy woman had to be Pamela's aunt. She leaned against a tall mustached man in a three-piece suit.

AT LAST THE door swung open to reveal the judge. He rearranged his papers, rapped his gavel, and began again. "Mr. Eriksson, from what I've seen today, you seem to be an honest man. One who would not want to bring harm or destruction to anyone or anything. We *could* reduce the sentence to minor trespassing."

The ladies in the back murmured in concerned whispers.

"Although apparently the library staff did know you were residing there on the property," he continued. "Consequently, your sentence will be removed completely after donation of one large painting to be displayed in the courtroom foyer." The judge looked at Finn with the slightest of smiles. "Yes, although I have refused to let it sway me, I am quite aware of your artistic talent."

An eruption of cheerful murmuring came from behind us—not from the Johnson relatives, but further back, where the artists were. I let out a small clap accidentally and then quickly sat on my hands. I watched Finn raise his chin as his eyes went wide. For the first time that day he looked to where we were sitting and nodded. My smile felt so huge, my face ached.

Pamela and Claire had both gone wide-eyed, as well. They sat very straight in their matching crisp-collared shirts, like obedient school girls on the first day of class.

"As for you, Pamela Johnson, and Claire Tibbetts," continued the judge. "I know you're from good families; however, there are limits to what you can get away with. Please see me after court for your lengthy community service assignments." Then he added wryly, "We'll find you something pleasant to do. . .for example, scrubbing the park district toilets."

Cat gave my hand a quick squeeze. "Yes!" she mouthed.

The judge looked pointedly at Pamela and Claire. "And if I ever see either one of you on this stand again, you can believe I will not be easy on you a second time."

He banged his gavel. "Case closed."

We all rushed to the lobby, and soon Finn was surrounded with well-wishers.

"No excuse now, Finn," shouted out one of the Arts and Crafts ladies. "You'll *have* to become a member." And then this same lady, a blonde woman with bright red lips, did an amazing thing. As though Finn were the most handsome, eligible bachelor in the world, she blew him a kiss. Which, of course, made his face turn scarlet.

22

AFTER SCHOOL THE next day, I raced down to the pier and found Finn already packing up. He looked years younger than I'd seen him in weeks. Because the exhibit had gone well, Finn had a few commissions for more pictures, plus, of course, the request for a large courthouse painting would keep him busy. However, my afternoons watching him work were numbered. The sun set earlier and earlier as we moved towards the end of October. And next week, after daylight savings ended, there would probably be no light at all by the time the school bus dumped me off.

I soaked up the view of the gray sea rolling in, while gulls dipped into its frothy peaks. I already regretted those days when a snow blizzard might keep me inside, away from this scene. Sure, others might claim it too, but this would always be my special place, my ocean.

The court case proved justice could be served and Finn's problems—solved. And now that the trial was over, a great weight had fallen from *my* shoulders, as well. Even my bus rides home would improve, what with Pamela and Claire having to stay in town for their community service. I'd begun to think of Finn as my lucky penny and wondered if his good fortune might rub off on me.

"Ya know that little problem I had?" I grinned at the memory of his comment. "The one where I looked like a nervous old tom cat?"

Finn immediately stopped rolling up brushes into a paint-stained cloth. He motioned to his little stool. "Sit down and tell me what's going on," he encouraged.

I sat, and before I knew it, I'd spilled the beans about the whole Craig versus Ricky situation.

"Now, that is a problem. Don't you worry. It'll sort itself out." He took a step back from his painting and then scraped off a minuscule slice with his fingernail. "You're not picking one out to marry, are you?"

I laughed. "Of course not."

"Nothing to worry about then." Finn twisted the top of the turpentine bottle to make sure it was on tight.

I felt kind of silly. Here I had spit my whole life story out and all he could say was, "don't worry?" He had listened with his full attention, but now it was back to business as usual. How could I not worry? There was only a short time left for me to decide who I should go to the dance with, and if I didn't figure out soon who I liked best, I'd go crazy. Sure, Craig was super cool, but Ricky was cute, too, and lately I'd felt more like I could be myself with him. I guess sometimes I felt kind of babyish with Craig, like I was still stuck in the sandbox while he was swinging from the monkey bars.

Waves from a distant speed boat slapped against the pier supports. Figuring he'd already forgotten I was there, I got up to leave when Finn suddenly said, "I can remember my first dance."

That got my attention. It was hard to picture grizzly ol' Finn at a school dance. He smoothed the hairs of his favorite brush into a fine point and then placed it into the cloth with the other tools while I waited for him to go on.

"I went with a gal named Clara." Finn grinned. Then he frowned. "No, wait a minute. I *wanted* to go with Clara, but I ended up with Grace. I think that was her name—a redheaded girl. My, my, she knew how to have a good time." He checked the cap of each tube of paint and continued to share bits and pieces of his memories. "That was the first time I heard "By the Beautiful Sea," a mighty nice tune." Finn hummed a few bars, and I recognized it as one my mother sometimes sang, as well.

While Finn reminisced, I realized that although it was important enough for him to remember fifty or sixty years later, the details didn't really matter any-more. It was obviously a pleasant memory whether he had gone with Clara *or* Grace.

"Thanks, Finn." I looked him in the eyes with a huge smile on my face. "You've been a big help."

"I have?" He appeared puzzled as he stroked the whiskers on his chin.

"Yep." I turned to go. "And in a couple of weeks, I'll tell you all about my first dance, too."

ON THURSDAY, I ran down to the pier to meet Cat. I knew Finn wouldn't be around today—much too cold for painting. Clusters of colorful autumn leaves struck the ground and then lifted and swirled again with each new breeze. They crunched under my steps. Pretty soon the first snowflakes would fall. Winter struck early in the Port—sometimes covering the pumpkins with snow by Halloween. I zipped up my jacket and inhaled a big gulp of crisp sea air. The ocean was dead gray, straight to the horizon.

Cat stood staring out to sea at the end of the wharf. She didn't see me at first, and I noticed the expression of her profile seemed kind of sad. She'd been catching up on a science project, so we hadn't had a chance to talk since the trial.

"Hi, Cat, you okay?"

She turned the rest of the way around and laughed. Her familiar cheerful face was back in place. "Did you figure out what you're wearing to the dance?" she asked.

Good old Cat. That was one of the reasons I liked her as much as I did. She never went moping around, complaining about her own problems.

I smiled. "I was thinking we should both wear our yellow sweaters, the ones that almost match."

She shook her head. "I'm not going."

"Why?"

"Because I don't feel like walking in by myself. Everybody's pairing up. I mean, even you have two dates."

Poor Cat. She had been so excited about the dance, and I felt I'd let her down. "You *have* to go, or else I'll be by myself."

She looked at me, puzzled.

"I'm not going with Ricky *or* Craig. I decided the whole situation is ridiculous. I'm too young to be worried about boys. This is my first dance and I want to have fun. With you, my best friend." As I spoke, Cat's face brightened with every word. "It's up to me, right, my choice? I figure I might as well choose myself and how *I* want to do things."

"You mean, you're going to say no to Ricky?" She bit her lip. "He'll be crushed."

I'd been so busy thinking about everything, I'd blocked out that problem. Now, I pictured him having to go to the dance alone. Or worse, sitting home building his ship model. I remembered how lonely I felt last spring when I stayed home wondering if Craig was at the Twist Twirl dance. No way could I leave either one of them home this time. "I know what we can do. Let's get both Craig and Ricky to go with us. The four of us can walk in together." I began to giggle. "We'll be a gang."

Cat rolled her eyes and joined in my laughter. "A gang of misfits!"

"Nope. We'll be a perfect fit." Puffs of cold vapor were escaping from our happy smiles. I jumped up and down a few times to get warm. "Now. What should we wear?"

We spent the next half hour figuring out our outfits. Nancy would have been proud. My mind was full and happy as I headed home under the cold dark sky.

THE NEXT MORNING at the bus stop, Ricky agreed to our plan to attend the dance as a group, with only one hesitation.

"Are you sure Craig should go with us? He's kind of full of himself, isn't he?"

171

"You'll like him fine once you get to know him," I said.

Ricky didn't look convinced. He pushed up his glasses, which he always did before he forced himself to say something. "Can you dance mostly with me?"

"Oh, okay. Sure." Gosh, I hadn't thought about actually dancing with either one of them. Maybe Craig didn't dance.

LATER THAT DAY, Craig pulled me aside in the school hallway. I'd been busy studying for a math test between classes and hadn't been able to give him an answer yet. "Well?" he said.

"Meet me at the pier after school," I whispered, right before a big group of kids passed by us.

That afternoon, I reached the pier first. I glanced over at the beach. Finn's boat wasn't there. I had a feeling he wouldn't be painting again until spring. But he'd be back. That I was sure of. He still had several pictures to complete and had even agreed to add Pup to one of his seascapes. The courthouse painting would be done on the island—a distant view of Port Wells at sunset. As word traveled, Finn would probably have more orders than he could fill. I looked across to the island, hoping to see wisps of smoke coming from his chimney. Unfortunately, his hut was on the opposite side of the lighthouse with no trace of smoke in sight.

I turned back to watch Craig arrive. Gosh, he was handsome. His hair shone in the sunlight, and his cheeks were ruddy from the raw air.

I began babbling like I always did in his presence, about how I didn't want to let Cat down and how Ricky had asked me first, and blah, blah, blah.

"Hang on," said Craig. "You're making me dizzy. So. You want to go as friends, right? The four of us? Us two and the nerdy Fantinis?"

I peeked up at him and then nodded slowly. "Their name is Fantino, and they're not nerdy."

"Great. No problem."

I looked up into those blue, blue eyes. "You don't mind?"

"Nope." He grinned. "I hadn't exactly figured out how we'd get there anyway. But, hey, if your dad wants to drive, let's go for it." Then his eyes flickered away from my face towards the water. His brow creased in concentration. "Well, what do ya know." Craig's face lit up happier than I'd ever seen him.

I turned around and followed his gaze. "Pup? It's Pup!"

We raced down to the beach and watched the little seal swim in. His pal followed behind. It seemed to be the same seal I had seen Pup with the last time. She was slightly smaller and darker than Pup, and I liked to think of her as his girlfriend. We met them at the shoreline. At first, Pup was hesitant.

"Aw, come on," said Craig. "You know we're old friends."

"Here, Pup," I called. I reached out and drew him in close, up onto the sand. His little heart-shaped marking begged for a kiss and I gave him one. I inhaled his warm fishy smell.

Craig patted the small sleek head. "You've grown some." Then Craig held him like he'd never let him go. He continued to whisper in soft, husky tones. His face was turned away from me, focused on Pup, and I wondered if he might be crying. "I missed you, little buddy."

It was perfect having the three of us here together again. Pup's friend kept her distance until Pup returned to her side. Then they both swam out further than we could follow with our eyes. But it was okay now. Pup could come and go without me getting upset because that's how life is. Everything was how it should be. Pup belonged in the ocean and had never looked more content. I was happy now, too, with friends and fun stuff to look forward to.

I studied Craig for a minute as he continued to watch the water. Even though he seemed more worldly since last spring, in times like these, it was as though nothing had changed. Was it all in my imagination, and he wasn't growing away from me after all? Then I remembered to ask him what had been niggling at the corner of my mind all week. "I think I saw you at the football game last Saturday. With Pamela and Claire and some older kids. I think they were smoking." I watched his face.

He looked away and shook his head. "Nope, wasn't me." Then he moved back from the shoreline.

How strange. It was almost like he was lying. Why couldn't he look at me when he answered? And even more importantly, why would he lie to *me?* Maybe I'd been too slow making my decision, or he had already known I was going to say no. Maybe he liked some other girl now. Confused, I decided it best to shrug it off.

I kicked a little clump of seaweed along the sand with my sneaker. "Thanks for understanding about the dance."

"No, problemo." Craig started heading up the road, and then shouted back over his shoulder. "Just be sure you dance with me more than that other blockhead!"

23

I ALWAYS LOVED to dress up on Halloween and, of course, get candy. When Nancy saw me rummaging through costumes, she said, "There's no way you can go trick or treating again this year, Amy. You're in high school now. Trick or treat is for little kids."

"Of course," I said. Inside I wanted to scream: But it's *Halloween!*

I watched the clock that evening as darkness fell. Because we were on a hill, the few kids who lived in the Port never bothered to climb up to our door for one little piece of candy. There were much more productive neighborhoods on the other side of town. One year we did have two kids. The following year, I sat ready with a big bowl of Milky Ways, but nobody showed up.

Despite Nancy's comment, I poked through the costume box again, anyway. At the bottom was an ugly witch's mask. I tried it on in front of my mirror. It hid my face entirely. Then I pulled up the hood of my sweatshirt to cover my hair. Not bad. I grabbed my old striped afghan and wrapped it around my shoulders, admiring myself in the mirror.

Don't do this. Don't do that. I'd been listening to Nancy tell me what to do for far too long. I shouldn't have to miss out just because she didn't appreciate Halloween. True, I'd certainly done a lot of growing up this past year, but that didn't mean I was too big to have fun. Ever since meeting Finn, I seemed to have even more courage to be who I chose to be. Not who someone else thought I should be. *Me?* I loved creeping around on Halloween!

I opened my bedroom door a crack and listened. Mom and Nancy laughed at something on TV. A moment later, my father cleared his throat. Perfect! Everyone accounted for in the living room. I crept down the stairs to the front door and slid it open.

"I'm going to Cat's house, back in a while," I shouted over my shoulder. I pulled the door shut behind me and ran down the hill in the dusky night. It was only a little tricky to see through the large cutout eyes of my mask.

When I arrived on the Fantinos' doorstep, I waited a few seconds to slow my breathing. I could see right through the window and into their lighted living room. Ricky was sprawled out on the floor watching TV, and Cat was behind him, reading a book on the sofa. Their parents must have been in another room. I watched a moment, enjoying the cozy scene. Then I reached up and gave their ship bell a good shake.

Cat and Ricky both jumped up and I could hear their rushed footsteps in the hall as they neared the entrance. Ricky yanked the door open, his head peering around the side of it. Through the opening I could see Cat fumbling with the candy dish to make sure it showed a good variety on top.

"Trick or Treat!" I said in a shaky, squeaky, little witch voice.

"Oh, you're scary," said Ricky, playing along as if to a child.

Cat held the dish low so I could select a treat. "What a great costume! Do you live nearby?"

I nodded. "Hmm, I love M&Ms," I said, still using my witch voice. "Can I have more?"

"Oh." Cat appeared flustered. "Of course." She picked up the dish again and then paused. She shot Ricky a look that said, "She could at least say thank you."

I gave a few slow shakes of my head, back and forth to show my impatience. I tried like anything to not let my giggles be heard.

Ricky and Cat exchanged looks again.

"Hey, wait a minute," said Ricky. I peered through my eye slots to see him pointing at my lime-green sneakers. "Those look familiar."

Cat's mouth fell open. "Amy?"

I whipped off my mask and erupted in laughter. They joined me.

"Oh, my gosh," I said. "You should have seen your faces."

"We were hoping *someone* would come by tonight," said Ricky.

"Only you could get away with this, Amy," said Cat. "Sh. . .."

"Don't say it!" I shouted.

"Gosh, I was only going to say short people can pass for younger, ya know, because of your height."

"Oh, okay. That's fine." I laughed. "I was afraid you were going to dredge up my old nickname." Until recently with Pamela, it had been a long time since anyone had called me Shrimp, and of course, Cat wouldn't, but every once in a while I'd remember how it felt. Not that it was the most horrible word, but kids like Pamela and Claire always said it with such scorn in their voices.

"Nope. Before our time." Cat put the candy dish back on the hall table and then changed the subject. "Oh, yeah, Amy, I'm glad you came by. I wanted to ask if you could fill in for me on Saturday."

My mood sank a bit. "Story time?"

179

Cat nodded.

"Of course," I said, even though I dreaded the idea.

"Are you sure you don't mind?" she said.

I crossed my fingers behind my back. "It would be a pleasure."

Ricky still lingered around the doorway. "Wanna come in and hang out?" he said.

"No, I'd better get back. Maybe I'll trick or treat at my house, too, and see if they know me." We all laughed, and I was on my witchy way.

CONSEQUENTLY, ON SATURDAY, for the second time that fall, I found myself stuck filling in for Cat again at story time. I decided not to worry about it and, thus, I showed up at the same time as the kids. Today, there were five. Their parents organized them on the rug and then went off to browse the library stacks.

"Hi, kids!" I said, as loud and jolly as I could muster. "Cat will be back later. We can tell her all about the fun we had."

"I remember you," said a boy. Uh, oh, I thought to myself as an unpleasant recollection passed through my mind. He was the one who hadn't liked my book choice.

"I remember you, too," I said cheerfully.

"Can you read the little engine book?" he said.

"Really?"

He nodded. His eyes never left my face, and I wondered if he thought, or hoped, he was messing up my plans by asking for the same story. A curly-haired girl, another child I remembered only too well, began to chant. "Engine, engine, engine."

I grabbed the book off the shelf—thank goodness it wasn't checked out—and started right in, making sure to show the pictures to everyone before I turned the pages.

The little girl who had cried last time, moved closer to me on the rug.

"I think I can. I think I can!" we all shouted to help the little engine.

Once I forgot about myself and concentrated only on how to make it the best story the kids had ever heard, everything went great. It might not be my thing, and I'd never be as good at storytelling as Cat was, but I'd gotten through just fine.

AFTER THE CHILDREN were reconnected with their parents, I went over to Miss Cogshell's big chair in the back and relaxed for a few minutes with one of the new books I'd recently discovered—*Techniques of Novel Writ-*

ing, by a guy named Burack. I'd also learned that some of the universities had great creative writing programs. I laughed to think how silly I'd been over the last few weeks. There were more important things to worry about than which boy I should go to a high school dance with. Other girls could continue to make it a priority if they chose. However, now that I'd figured out my college plans, I couldn't afford to be a fluff-head. I would be picky with my time and concerns.

Even with all my big talk, though, I was still jumping out of my skin with excitement for the dance.

24

As sure as pumpkins ripen on the vine, the night of the Fall Harvest Dance arrived.

I was all ready to go an hour before dinner. Mom didn't always cook big meals, and we sometimes had to forage for ourselves; however, tonight was one of my favorites: spaghetti and meatballs.

"Sketti ready?" I teased. Ever since I was a little kid I'd been asking her that.

"Not even started." Mom filled up the large pasta pot with water. "I'll get going. You've got a big night." She turned towards me and smiled. "Don't you look nice."

Nancy came into the kitchen. "Is that what you're wearing?" She had a movie date that night and was looking forward to her own dance the following weekend—a homecoming dance for the upper grades. Because our school's gym wasn't very big, it made sense to split the dances into two age groups.

I looked down at my yellow sweater and plaid bell-bottoms and nodded.

"Well, I guess your outfit's fine, but what about your hair?"

I fiddled with the ends hanging down beyond my shoulders. "What about it?"

"It's the same as always. You look like that every day."

I shrugged.

"Come on," she said. "I'll fix it."

She steered me up to her room and plunked me down in front of her mirrored vanity table. I'd never sat on the little tufted stool before—it was pretty comfortable. I decided to let her mess around with my hair for a few minutes.

I watched Nancy in the mirror as she grabbed supplies—comb, clips, electric rollers. She separated my hair into sections and quickly spun them into two rows of curlers. "Okay, now we'll time it." She studied her watch with one hand on her hip. I fiddled with some of her colorful little bottles.

"Good idea, let's do your nails, too, while we wait." I yanked back my hands. "Hmm," she said. "What color?"

"Do you have any yellow?" I said.

"Yuck. We'll go with this one—Cotton Candy. It's good for younger kids. Hold still, we only have a few more minutes before I take out the curlers."

I rolled my eyes and let her pull my hand into place. She expertly coated each nail with the pale pink color.

"Phew," I shouted. "I forgot how much nail polish stinks!"

"Relax. Almost done. Now, wave your hands back and forth, and they'll dry in no time." She checked her watch. "Perfect, one more minute."

It ended up being kind of fun. When Nancy was away from her crowd and not worrying about how popular she was, she became the Nancy I used to know when we were little—two sisters hanging out together.

"Sketti's ready," called Mom from downstairs.

With nimble fingers, Nancy slipped all the heated rollers out of my hair. I looked in the mirror and made a face. Separate coils of hair covered my head. The type of ringlets you wanted to snap your finger at and say boing.

"We'll fluff it later," said Nancy.

"Get it while it's hot," shouted Mom.

"Cute!" said Mom as I entered the kitchen. "You look like Shirley Temple."

I rolled my eyes. "It's not finished. If my hair doesn't end up looking ten times better than this, I'll be staying home."

"It's going to look great," said Nancy.

I tucked a large napkin into the neckline of my sweater to keep the red sauce from ruining my outfit and then ate as much as my nervous stomach could hold.

After dinner, we fluffed my hair, and I even let Nancy talk me into a little pale lipstick. Without comment, she dabbed a couple of tiny globs of concealer on my face as well, making any blemishes invisible. I suppose it could have been the lighting playing tricks on me, but I couldn't take my eyes off the pretty girl looking back at me in the mirror.

CAT AND RICKY walked over to meet us at the car. Cat had her yellow sweater on to match mine, and Ricky was all spruced up in a crisp, collared shirt. Stars sparkled through the tops of the pine trees. At first I worried Craig would be late, but then he stepped out from under the stars at the last minute. He looked the same as always—jeans and a sweatshirt—apart from his hair, which was combed back and shiny.

Dad drove us to the school. When we rode by the pier, I gasped with appreciation for the full moon that hung still and bright over the water, its beams floating in on dark waves. I pointed it out to the others. Naturally, they had already admired the moon on their walk to my house. With all the pine trees on our hill, it wasn't the best place for sky gazing.

I was in the front seat with Dad while Cat sat between Craig and Ricky. Cat's mom would pick us up at ten-thirty. Did that mean I'd be between the two boys on the ride home? Weird. Don't think about it, I told myself.

I glanced back at them once and was startled to see Craig's eye wink at me. I kept my gaze forward after that and wondered, had I seen that, or imagined it? I'd never seen him wink before, I mean, who knew, maybe he had developed a nervous twitch.

WE ENTERED THE gym right as they dimmed the lights. A silver ball spun overhead. It scattered sparkling, swirling beams everywhere—walls, floor, ceiling—even on our faces.

"Far out!" said Cat. "What is that thing?"

"I don't know." I pulled my eyes away. "Makes me kind of dizzy."

"I saw one of those disco balls in Boston," said Craig. Then he looked me up and down.

"What?" I glanced at my shirt. "Do I have spaghetti sauce on me? No matter how careful I was I knew I'd end up with at least one. . ."

"Shhh," said Craig. "You look fantastic."

I looked away and tried to hide my grin.

The gym truly was transformed. Orange crepe paper and large harvest moons hung from the gym's rafters. It was hard to picture sweaty basketball games in the same space. Other than a small group of girls and one couple, nobody danced. We all stared at the couple. The girl had her hands clasped around the back of the boy's neck. His arms sat low at her waist. They shuffled in little circles. It certainly looked easy enough.

"Amy, let's go to the girls' room," said Cat.

I was about to say I didn't need to go, but caught her look in the nick of time.

We dashed to the restroom to find a line already formed. "What is it?" I asked my friend.

"Ricky keeps staring at you," said Cat in a whisper. "I think he's going to ask you to dance. He wants to beat Craig. Before we got to your house, he said he wished Craig wasn't going and that I should talk to him a lot. To keep him busy." She rolled her eyes. "So, I wanted to save you. You look really cute tonight, by the way. Your hair is gorgeous."

"You look great, too, Cat." Her usual long braid was coiled up at the back of her neck. A daisy-shaped hair barrette was stuck above the bun.

"The flower was my mom's idea. Probably looks stupid, but that's never stopped me before."

"I envy you that."

"*You* envy me?"

"Yeah, you always seem confident and unafraid. Well, except for when you hear noises in the trees on a hike." We both laughed remembering how Cat had jumped a mile when Finn threw a rock into the woods.

I grinned at our faces in the girls' room mirror. "I think I might try dancing."

Cat pulled back and looked me in the eyes. "Really? In front of everyone? Well, this is one thing you're braver at than me. I'm such a klutz."

"Nancy and I used to practice waltzing when we were little. She needed a partner, and there I was."

Cat looked at me with what I guess I'd call admiration and then shrugged. "Go for it then!" Her look changed to panic as we moved up to become the front of the line. "But wait, what am I supposed to do while you're dancing?" She laughed. "Looks like I'll be drinking a lot of punch."

As we headed back to our spot in the gym, "Joy to the World" came on. Cat and I looked at each other, with wide smiles, as we sang out the first lyrics about a bullfrog named Jeremiah. Then I saw both Craig and Ricky coming straight at me. Craig was kind of sauntering, cool as always, but his eyes didn't leave my face. Ricky was biting his lip. He did a little skip, hop, to get around people, and ahead of Craig.

I wondered whether to make another run for the girls' room, as I watched my two would-be dance partners draw near.

25

RICKY REACHED ME first. "Want to dance?"

"Oh. To this?"

"Sure." Ricky took my hand and pulled me over to the now crowded dance floor. I looked around and tried to copy some of the moves. I thought of a recent American Bandstand show where *Three Dog Night* performed the song live while all the kids danced. They made dancing look easy on TV. Somehow I couldn't catch the beat. Shuffling and swaying seemed to be good enough though, so I shuffled back and forth self-consciously, and Ricky did the same.

I glanced over to where we had left Craig and Cat. Where were they? Oh. Wow. They were doing some sort of crazy swing dancing. Craig seemed to be making it up as they went, pulling a red-faced, giggling Cat along beside him. I caught Ricky's eye and nodded at Cat and Craig. Ricky turned to look. Then we both laughed, happy they were having fun.

Everyone around us was going wild with the song. Pamela and Claire, in matching glittery hot-pants, were doing some foolish new dance, bumping their hips against each other. A group of boys circled them and cheered them on. Ever since the trial, except in class, I hadn't seen much of those two girls. They were still completing their many hours of community service, and I hoped the experience would turn out two nicer people.

When the song ended, a new one began. Craig and Cat galloped over to join us, and the four of us danced to a bunch of tunes. We took a few breaks for punch and chips, but otherwise danced the night away. It was great. None of us seemed to care what anybody else thought. And believe me, we tried some *funky* dance moves. The whole school was doing the same. A couple of sophomore girls asked Craig to dance, although he always came back to us after.

As I danced with Cat and Ricky, I studied Craig's partners carefully and wondered how he knew these girls. Or *did* he know them? Did I recognize them from the football game group? I wasn't sure. Finally, I pulled my eyes away. I had made my decision not to have a date all to myself and watching them wasn't helping me enjoy that choice.

Between songs, a tall kid came over and asked Cat to dance. She glowed as they moved out onto the dance floor. I recognized him as the boy, Jeremy I think, whom she sometimes walked with after their shared science class. They danced to a couple of songs and then he returned to his guy friends who hung out near the food.

Towards the end of the night, when we were all worn out and catching our breaths, the DJ said he was going to 'slow things down a little.' Ricky must have known what that meant because within seconds he was standing close enough for me to smell the French onion dip on his breath. He reached out to me as the first beautiful notes of "Color My World" sounded. Before I realized it, we were slow dancing.

"Having fun?" he asked.

I nodded and then snuck a peek back at the others—anything to stop from staring blankly into Ricky's eyes, a few inches above mine. Craig and Cat appeared to be in the middle of some big discussion, as they edged off the dance floor. Ricky and I continued stumbling back and forth to the slow beat. I tried like anything not to step on his feet.

"You look. . .," began Ricky.

"What?" The music was too loud for me to hear his soft voice.

Ricky chewed on his lip. "I only wanted to say you look really pretty tonight."

The dim lighting hid my blush. "Thanks," I managed.

Two songs later, Craig came up behind Ricky and tapped him on the shoulder.

"My turn," he said with a laugh.

Ricky gave a nervous nod, pushed up his glasses, and then walked away. I realized it wasn't exactly the right time to have a conversation, although it would have been nice if he didn't always clam up when Craig was around; if we could all be friends.

"I think I deserve at least the last dance," said Craig with a grin. His arm circled my waist and we danced to "Never My Love." I floated along as Craig's big hands tucked me in closer. My head fell right onto his shoulder like it belonged there. Where in the world had Craig learned to slow dance? In Boston? With whom? My mind spun to the rhythm of my suddenly graceful feet. Poor Ricky. He couldn't help it if he was shy. Like me.

Craig danced me across the floor to where it was more shadowy. A relief not to have as many flashing lights zooming past my eyes. Craig's voice softly sang along with the words. His breath tickled my ear and made my heart race.

Right as we hit the darkest spot on the floor, he bent his head down and kissed me. Fast, right on the lips. For a brief moment it was kind of fun, but then I pulled my head back, embarrassed, and more than a little uncomfortable. This wasn't how I'd imagined my first kiss, in the middle of a crowded gym floor. I thought it would happen a few years from now, maybe down by the water, under a full moon. This was all happening too fast for me.

Besides, I was with two guys tonight, what would Ricky think? With his hands on either side, Craig pulled my face back in close and did it again, pressing his lips hard against mine in a way I didn't like. I jerked back, startled. "Stop it!" I said, as the music ended and the lights flashed on.

With horribly perfect timing, my words had bolted into the silent pause of couples pulling apart to eye each other warily in the sudden brightness. At my shout, one or two kids looked over at us and I prayed they had all been minding their own beeswax up until that moment. Luckily, Ricky and Cat were all the way over on the other side of the gym.

"What's the matter?" said Craig.

I looked down embarrassed, taking a few more steps back. "Nothing," I finally said.

I began to shake—a habit that brought on even more humiliation. My lips tingled and I pictured my face—red as a beet. Obviously, Craig and I were on different paths—I was in the crosswalk and he was in the fast lane.

I snuck another peek at Craig. He had moved over a few yards after being summoned by a couple of the cool kids. In contrast to me, a bundle of nerves, his eyes sparkled in the bright lights and his teeth shined in his wide grin. He looked calm and confident as he returned to my side.

"Some of the kids said we could ride home with them," he said. "They're going to party down by the tracks for a while first."

Another party? Gosh, I was all tired out from this one. I'd heard stories of older kids having drinking parties down near the railroad tracks. "Huh, what kids?"

Craig pointed over his shoulder and I saw one of the girls he had danced with watching us.

I shook my head. "Not me. I'm going home with Cat and Ricky."

Craig brought his low voice down to my ear. "Are you sure?"

I nodded. "But you can. Go ahead if you want."

Craig seemed torn for a minute. However, I'm sure the last thing he wanted to do was drive home with Ricky's mommy, so off he went with a "Catch you later, Sunshine."

In a daze, I slowly moved back through the crowd towards Cat.

"There you are!" she sang out, relaxed and happy. "Come on. Mom's waiting. Where's Craig?"

I took a deep breath. "He's catching a ride with some other kids. I guess they live closer to him."

Cat rolled her eyes. "Hmpf, jumped ship, did he?"

She was right. Craig had made plans with us. It would have been wrong for us both to desert the Fantinos. I looked to see where Ricky was. He came up behind Cat. He met my eyes with a questioning look. I looked away.

ON THE RIDE home, I did indeed sit in the back, except now there was only one boy. I made myself as narrow as possible to prevent my legs from bumping into Ricky's.

Moonlight and streetlights flickered through the car windows. Cat's mom asked a zillion questions about the dance as she drove. Out of the corner of my eye, I saw Ricky's hand move towards me. I didn't want to hold hands with anyone. It felt wrong when I hadn't even been able to choose a date. I folded my hands into a tight fist on my lap. How could life suddenly have become so complicated? And when would this ride be over?

"Amy," Cat turned around and looked at me. "I just asked you if you liked the song selection."

"Oh! Yes. Yes, the music was great." How come I couldn't even remember most of them? All I could remember was that kiss and Craig's back as he walked away.

26

I FLOATED AROUND the house for the rest of the week-end, still under the spell of my first dance, *and* my first you-know-what. For some reason I blocked out the trip home. I mean just because Craig was offered another ride and bailed out on us, I shouldn't take it personally. Right?

ON THURSDAY, I was hanging out on the pier when Craig came by. When I heard his distinctive whistling, my first instinct was to hide, which of course, was ri-diculous. Not only would it solve nothing, but a quick glance over my shoulder showed he was already look-ing right at me. So, I continued to sit there. Seagulls circled the wharf. The dock boards squeaked behind me and memories of the very first time I talked with him, beyond the usual elementary school kid stuff, came flooding back to me. I could still see him in that old army jacket as he introduced me to Pup. I turned around and met his eyes.

"Hey, what's up?" he said moving into place beside me. His face was inches from mine. As close as when we'd...*stop!* I commanded myself.

Craig whistled a few bars of "Never My Love"—of all songs—and then apparently thinking better of it, cleared his throat. "Sorry about the other night."

I looked up at his sincere face. "You got home okay?"

Craig looked away and for the first time ever, he actually looked embarrassed. "Yep," he finally said. "Ya know, Amy. No matter what, I want to stay friends with you. For a long, long time."

I smiled. "Me, too."

"Well, naturally, you'd want to be friends with you." Craig laughed.

I shook my head. "I meant with you. Friends with you. For a long time."

"Sure, I'll be around."

We sat there quiet for a while. As usual Craig got fidgety first. "Hey, maybe when we're really old. Like twenty. Ya know after you've gone out with a bunch of schmucks. Maybe then we can try, well I don't know, something more serious."

I smiled. "Okay. It's a deal. But in the meantime, friends, right?"

Craig slapped me on the back. "Yep, you've got it right, buddy, old pal."

"OW!"

Craig looked concerned that he'd hurt me for about half a second. And then we both burst out laughing.

"And I'm still waiting on that song," I said.

"Ah, yeah." Craig thought a minute. "How about this?" He burst into a familiar tune except he changed most of the words to my name. "Amy, yeah yeah, Amy, yeah yeah."

I grinned. "Well, I guess it's a start." Happiness bubbled up inside me. It was great to know Craig and I could still be close friends even if he was way ahead of me in the romance department. It had always been his friendship I'd missed so strongly while he was away. And, who knew, maybe someday I'd be ready for the mushy stuff, too. For now, dating was still a ways off for me. I was in no rush.

I often thought of this girl, Francine, one of Pamela's cousins actually, who used to live across town. She was a few years older than Nancy and had fallen madly in love with some guy back when she was about my age. By the time she was sixteen, they had a kid and were living in a small trailer. Eventually the guy took off and now who knows where any of them ended up, but it was kind of sad that she never got to figure out who she was first—who she wanted to be in life.

It got dark early now and a bright crescent moon was already coming up over the horizon. Craig was still singing his crazy new song as we headed off in different directions. Him for home and me to the post office. I arrived a minute before Sally flipped the sign over to say closed. And what do you know, there was a letter for me!

Dear Amy,

Although deeply saddened to hear of Sylvia's passing, I was very pleased to receive a letter from you. Yes, we most certainly can be pen pals. It will be like holding onto a small piece of Sylvia, whom I already miss so dearly. She used to tell me a good deal about the goings on of the Port and I still yearn to visit there someday....

I finished reading the rest of Margie's message as I walked home, and then I read the full letter again. I couldn't wait to tell her all that had gone on these past few weeks.

THAT NIGHT AT supper my parents made an interesting announcement. "We've been thinking we'd like to invite Finn for Thanksgiving dinner," said Mom.

"Yes!" I said. "That's a great idea." I hadn't seen him for days and missed hearing his stories and watching his paintings come to life.

Nancy began to whine. "Does he have to come, Mom? He's not even family."

"Of course he should come," I said, already designing a card in my mind. "I'll make him an invitation and get it out on the next mail boat." The boat didn't run on weekends, but there would be one Monday morning.

Nancy sighed.

"That would be nice, Amy," said Mom. "Tell him to arrive by two."

"Okay." I poked at the green beans on my plate. "I guess Cat's family will be on their own, too. They usually go to their grandparents' house, except their grandparents will be away on a cruise this year."

Dad served himself another scoop of mashed potatoes. "The Fantinos are nice people," he said.

"Yes," said Mom. "I enjoyed talking with them at Finn's exhibit." My parents exchanged a look and then my mother said, "The last few holidays have been kind of quiet with only the four of us. And I do love a party." Years ago my grandparents and aunt and uncle always came for Thanksgiving, except now everyone but my uncle had passed on, and he was somewhere up in Canada.

I started to roll my eyes at my mother putting on her hostess-with-the-mostest voice; then I stopped short. Was she saying what I thought she was saying?

Mom threw her napkin onto the table and laughed. "Let's invite the Fantinos to our house for Thanksgiving!"

I dropped my fork to the floor with a crash. "The Fantinos *and* Finn?"

"We'll have quite the group." My father smiled. He neatly laid his fork across his plate and folded his napkin in his usual quiet way to set a good example for the rest of us.

I nearly jumped out of my seat with excitement to tell Cat and Ricky. And it's funny, I had to admit I found it kind of thrilling to picture Ricky at my family table. Snippets of our ride home from the dance had returned to me. And at least once a day I wondered how it would have felt if the two of us *had* held hands, alone in the back seat.

Ricky might not be as flashy as Craig, but he was a great kid, too, and about my speed—slowly making good choices for his future. Whereas with Craig, if I hadn't pulled in the reins, I might have gotten in way over my head, messing up my plans. And more than anything, I wouldn't want to risk our friendship. Not that I thought Craig would end up in ruins, but—I grinned to myself—I'd do my best to slow him down. Maybe we could even start studying together, like he used to do with Miss Cogshell.

"All four of them?" said Nancy, interrupting my thoughts.

"It's the least we can do to belatedly welcome the Fantinos to Port Wells," said Dad.

I grinned at Nancy and then ducked under the table to grab my fork. "Actually, there's five," I said as I popped back up. "Big brother Joey will be home on college break."

"Oh, brother," said Nancy. "Next you'll be asking the Miller kid, too."

"Craig's got plans. His whole family's going to be at his aunt's for a couple of days."

Dad stacked our dirty plates and put the silverware on top. Then he said, "Would you like to ask a friend, Nancy?"

"No. I'll see everybody at the homecoming game that morning. Besides I'm sure they'll all be with their own families like normal people. I'll eat fast and catch up with them again after."

I was busy planning in my head. "And then, while we're waiting for dinner, we could decorate apples to look like turkeys and put them around the table!"

"No way," said Nancy. "We've been doing that since we were little."

"It's a family tradition," I said. "We *need* to make them."

"Do you really think your high school friends and their *older* brother will play along? How embarrassing! Count me out." Nancy went over to the sink in a huff. It was her turn to do the dishes.

"Tell me what you need, Amy, and I'll add it to my grocery list," Mom said. "Oh, this is exciting!" Her face looked radiant. Mom loved to entertain. "Ten people will fit perfectly around the dining room table." She began to sort through tablecloths and napkins while I ran upstairs to make invitations.

27

THANKSGIVING DAY DAWNED bright and chilly. Smells of turkey and turnip wafted through the house all morning. Mom was in her element, bustling about the kitchen in her holiday apron. I made little name cards shaped like turkeys to put at each place setting. And then I stuffed dates with walnuts and rolled them in white powdered sugar. In a special long dish that had belonged to my grandmother, I put celery sticks with black olives nestled in the hollows. I was excited, though nervous, too. Would everything go all right? Would everyone get along okay?

FINN SHOWED UP a couple of minutes before two o'clock, sporting his sailboat tie. The first light snow-flakes were scattered over his worn tweed jacket.

"Brought a little something," he said, handing my mother a bulky brown paper bag.

Mom peeked inside. "Oh, roasted chestnuts! They smell wonderful, and still warm." She looked fondly at Finn. "This brings back memories of my childhood."

"For me, too, ma'am. Me, too."

The Fantinos arrived soon after, and then things really picked up.

"It's snowing!" yelled Cat before I finished getting the door open. Her cheeks glowed and snowflakes glistened in her dark hair. Mrs. Fantino carried a sweet potato casserole between two large potholder mitts. "I know I said we'd only bring cornbread and a pumpkin pie, but we couldn't get through Thanksgiving without one more of our family traditions," she said with a chuckle.

"My favorite," agreed her husband in a booming voice. "I could eat the whole pan!"

Cat said her father was like a new man now that he spent his workdays out on the ocean instead of stuck inside a city office building. And he certainly did look like a relaxed and happy lobsterman, dusting snow off his red plaid flannel shirt. Before the day was done, he insisted that we all come over to their house the following week for fresh lobster.

It was interesting to finally meet the fifth Fantino. Joey looked similar to Ricky, except he was taller and broader. And, as my father would say, he had the confidence of a college man. Nancy hadn't been home from the game long and still had her cheerleading outfit on. She stopped in her tracks to gaze up at him. "Are you Joey?"

"That's me," he said with a laugh. "You must be Nancy. Cat filled me in on the way over here."

I couldn't believe it, but I could've sworn Nancy blushed.

Although I'd spent ages planning out where everyone would sit at the table, after witnessing Nancy's reaction to Joey, I snuck into the dining room and swapped Joey and Ricky's name placards. Then I went back to the living room and joined the others.

"What's this?" Cat looked down at the supplies I'd set up on the coffee table.

Remembering Nancy's words, I suddenly felt embarrassed. "It's just a little craft. Kind of a tradition for the kids to do before dinner."

"Oh, I love crafts. Hey, Joey and Ricky, get over here. Amy's going to show us how to make these."

Joey picked up my sample apple. It had rows of gumdrops strung on toothpicks for the feathers, and a marshmallow head attached to the other end. "It looks like a turkey."

"Yeah, that's the idea," I said.

Ricky sat right down with his legs bunched up underneath him. "Are they decorations for the table?"

I nodded. With hopes rising, I watched Nancy inch closer.

She smoothed her shiny hair back over her shoulders. "Are you all really going to make these?"

"Sure," said Joey. "And I'm hoping I get to eat the whole thing after."

We all laughed and then Nancy and I joined them on the floor around the small table. "So, yeah," I said. "Here's what you do." I went through the easy steps. We began to put gumdrops onto toothpicks and then stuck them into our apples to make feathers.

All of us competed to make the best turkey ever, until we finally ran out of gumdrops. We added marshmallow heads and placed the turkeys near our name cards after finding our seats at the dining room table.

"What a beautiful setting," exclaimed Mrs. Fantino, as she sat down next to Mom.

It *was* beautiful. Nancy had been in charge of polishing all the dinnerware the night before. Our good china and silverware sparkled. Beams of light from the overhead chandelier reflected off the glassware. Every goblet had a lily-shaped folded napkin stuck inside. Through the bay window, snowflakes twinkled.

Mom and Dad each held a head of the table position—Dad so he could carve the turkey, and Mom so she could easily run back to the kitchen.

Finn found his place between me and Dad. He gave me a wink. "Looks like I've got a good spot."

"Me, too," said Joey with a laugh. Since he sat with Ricky on one side and Nancy on the other, his comment prompted a hair toss from Nancy. She gave him a sideways glance.

It seemed funny to be such a big part of this gathering. In the past I'd kept hidden away in my room while Mom and Dad had dinner parties.

When we were all settled into our seats, the overhead chandelier lights flickered three times. Would we lose power?

"Whew. Got the turkey cooked in time," said Dad. Everybody laughed. Mom lit the fancy pumpkin-colored table candles, just in case.

Cat sat on my other side, between me and Mrs. Fantino. She cleared her throat. "I wasn't sure if you'd be saying anything before your meal or not, but I brought a poem to share. A little gift, you know, to say thank you."

"How nice," said Mom. "Yes, please share."

"It's by Ralph Waldo Emerson." Cat cleared her throat again.

"Thanksgiving.

For each new morning with its light,

For rest and shelter of the night,

For health and food,

For love and friends,

For everything Thy goodness sends."

Out of the corner of my eye, I noticed Finn lift his napkin and quickly dab his cheek. When he spoke, his voice was gruff. "I'll tell ya all what I'm thankful for. If these two little gals hadn't been sticking their noses into my sorry existence, I'd be out on Wàwàckèchi right now, heating up a can of beans." He paused, shook his head, and laughed. "Either that or in jail."

A few chuckles sounded and then Dad said, "Very glad to have you, Finn."

Snow continued to fall silently outside the window. I pictured it piling up on pine boughs, drifting onto boats, and coating buoys—gently frosting the whole port in a safe layer of white. I looked around the table and studied the beloved faces of my friends. I thought of all the things I was thankful for—my family, meeting Cat and Ricky. And of course, Finn. Gosh, lots to be thankful for with those three. All fall I was desperate for Craig's return, for Craig's acceptance, maybe even for Craig's kiss, but now I realized something new. Even though Craig and I would continue to be friends, hopefully for a very long time, I was most thankful for the self-confidence to make my own choices. And I'd found that on my own.

After all my adventures over the last months I felt I could handle whatever this life handed me. I even felt thankful for good ol' Mrs. Baldwin and especially for my treasured memories of Miss Cogshell and Pup. Why, I even had a new pen pal and all sorts of plans for college someday. I looked around once more and felt truly blessed. Everything I'd wanted was right beside me, or maybe inside me, all along. No need to make a wish on the wishbone this year. And I certainly didn't need to jump up and announce these feelings that filled me from head to toe. But looking around that table of friendly faces, I knew I could have spoken, out loud and from my heart, if I had chosen to.

About the Author

Marcia Strykowski is a children's book author who also works at a public library. One of the perks of her job is she often comes home with a stack of new juvenile fiction to devour. Marcia lives in New England with her family and is a member of the Society of Children's Book Writers and Illustrators. *Amy's Choice,* a companion novel to *Call Me Amy,* is her second novel for children.